Alaric put his hands on the dome. When he felt a tingling in his palms, he thought nothing of it, but he couldn't ignore the excruciating pain that seared through him immediately afterward. His hands flew from the Folly, but the pain did not lessen. If anything it intensified, doubling him over. It lasted no more than fifteen or twenty seconds, but so acute was the agony that when it began to recede he remained hunched over, eyes tight shut, fearing its return. But then something touched his cheek. Something damp and very cold. He opened his eyes. Flakes of snow danced about his head. He stared about him, too numb to be astonished. He was in the south garden, under the Family Tree. What am I doing here? he thought. I should be indoors, in the River Room, not—

MICHAEL LAWRENCE

A CRACK IN THE LINE

THE WITHERN RISE TRILOGY · VOLUME I

A GREENWILLOW BOOK

HarperTempest

An Imprint of HarperCollins*Publishers*

A Crack in the Line
Copyright © 2003 by Michael Lawrence
First published in 2003 in Great Britain by
Orchard Books.
First published in 2004 in the United States by
Greenwillow Books.

Library of Congress Cataloging-in-Publication Data
Lawrence, Michael.
A crack in the line / by Michael Lawrence.
p.   cm.
"Greenwillow Books."
Summary: Sixteen-year-old Alaric discovers how to travel to an alternate reality, where his mother is alive and his place in the family is held by a girl named Naia.
ISBN-10: 0-06-072479-X (pbk.)
ISBN-13: 978-0-06-072479-5 (pbk.)
[1. Space and time—Fiction.   2. England—Fiction.]
I. Title.
PZ7.L43675Cr 2004   2003056860
[Fic]—dc22

Typography by Chad W. Beckerman
❖
First paperback edition, 2005
Visit us on the World Wide Web!
www.harperteen.com

For May and Ron Knight
and the host of others
who knew and loved W.B.
all those years ago

I shall be telling this with a sigh
Somewhere ages and ages hence:
Two roads diverged in a wood, and I—
I took the one less traveled by,
And that has made all the difference.

Robert Frost, "The Road Not Taken"

The most beautiful thing we
can experience is the mysterious.
It is the source of all true art
and science.

Albert Einstein

Part ①

Lexie's Folly

_____Day Seven

At sixteen, Alaric and Naia were as alike as any two people of opposite sexes can be. They had the same dark eyes and hair, same long straight nose, wide mouth—even the same slightly crooked front tooth. But it wasn't looks alone. Far from it. They shared a history, a lineage, memories, and had lived all their lives in the same house, Withern Rise, where they had occupied the same room, done the same things, more often than not had the same thoughts at the very same instant. And yet . . .

They had never met.

Hadn't the faintest inkling of each other's existence.

They knelt at their windows, on their beds—same window, same bed, unknown and invisible to each other—gazing out at the same water, trees, February sky. The boat landing below the garden was opaque with frost and the river toiled beneath shifting plates of ice. Snow was falling. The first soft white splodges thumped the window; clung to the glass for anxious seconds before losing their grip and slithering downward.

But while watching identical snow strike identical windows, Alaric's and Naia's circumstances could not have been more different. The central heating, for one thing. The central heating in both houses had been installed in the same hour twenty-eight years earlier, but while at Naia's the system was regularly serviced, the one at Alaric's hadn't been serviced for almost three years, with the result that the boiler had packed up five days ago. Her room, therefore, was snug and warm, while for Alaric, fully dressed within the fat cloak of his duvet, it felt as cold indoors as it looked out.

Then, suddenly, another difference. A movement, across the river from his window but not hers. In the ragged clump on the opposite bank, a man stepped from cover. He was thin, elderly, a bit seedy looking in a shapeless black overcoat, and he simply stood there, staring at the house. Probably harmless, Alaric thought; some nosey parker with nothing better to do on a cold winter morning. But you never knew. He might be casing the joint. There'd been a lot of break-ins around here lately.

"Al, I'm off now!"

His father's voice, downstairs, trying hard to sound light. They'd argued ferociously last night. Things had gotten out of hand, ending with recriminatory shouts, slammed doors, rages in separate rooms. The echo of the row filled the morning house like bad air. Alaric waited for the call to be repeated before discarding the duvet and sidling out to glare down from the galleried landing. His father, a dwarf in the hall far below, smiled tautly up at him, keen not to part on bad terms.

"Have to go, son."

He went down, heavy footed, face set in an unforgiving mask, no immediate plans to put their estrangement behind him. The house seemed to get colder and colder the lower he went. His hostility also increased with every step. His father sensed this.

"Al—look—try and see it from my point of view. I have a life too, you know. And think of Kate. It won't be easy for her either, at first."

He didn't give a damn about Kate. "Do you know what day it is?" he asked sharply. His father's frown said it all. "That's what I thought."

A difficult pause, until: "You've got my mobile number?"

"Yeah."

"Not that you'll need it. Liney'll be here soon, if she doesn't end up in a ditch. Driver from hell, that woman. If she makes it, she'll sort out anything that needs sorting."

"I don't need a baby-sitter," Alaric said bitterly.

His father snatched up the overnight bag at his feet.

"We've been over that. You're still a minor, which means I'm still responsible for you. You'll have to put up with her." He softened his tone, with effort. "It's only a couple of days anyway." Attempted a smile. "Come and see me off?"

They walked down the long, cold hallway that ran from the rear of the house to the front door. Actually, they walked from the original front to the original back, the two main entrances having been effectively reversed since the 1930s. In 1884, when Withern was built, the river was a commercial and social highway. Most visitors from beyond Eynesford and the adjoining market town of Stone came by boat. The river frontage of the house was moderately impressive back then. The brickwork was brighter, there were painted shutters at the windows, and the door, set into a quarry-tiled porch, was reached via a flight of steps from the boat landing below. The porch and steps and landing were still there, but the shutters had been removed long since. A pair of somber yews guarded the porch and ivy scrambled across the walls, but the house looked rather plain these days—especially in winter, from the river.

"I could do without this," his father said, opening the door to a gust of snow. "Just hope it's only local, that's all."

He scooped the bottle of milk from the step and handed it over like a parting gift, then flipped up the collar of his old brown bomber jacket. Part of the collar stayed down. Alaric didn't tell him.

"I'll give you a ring when I get there. Sometime this evening."

Alaric shut the door the moment his father was off the step but remained where he was, listening for the distant creak of the garage doors and the forty-year-old Daimler growling to life, slow tires on gravel as it reversed out, and finally the deep-throated toot as the car plunged into the avenue of trees that swept all the way to the gate.

And then he was alone, in a house as cold and still as an empty church. He went through to the kitchen and put the bottle of milk in the fridge, cursing his life, his luck, his world. Before the morning was out, his hyperactive aunt would be there, filling the place with her inane racket and absurd ways, and in a couple of days his father would return with his lousy fancy woman and nothing—nothing!—would ever be the same again.

He was right about that. After today, nothing would be the same. But not because of anything his aunt or his father or Kate Faraday did. All of his darkest and wildest imaginings could never have prepared him for the things that were about to happen to him.

Things that he and no one else would set in motion.

7.2

Alex handed her husband his winter coat. He protested that he couldn't drive all that distance in a bloody great thing like that. She reminded him that it was cold out. He reminded *her* that he would be in the car.

"It'll be cold in the car till it warms up," she said. "You can pull over and take it off when you're warm enough."

"This is like living with Mother," Ivan said.

"Your mother wouldn't have put up with all this argument."

He put the coat on. She was buttoning him up and smoothing him down before he'd gotten the second arm in. He shook her off.

"Will you leave me *alone*, woman?"

"You look a mess," she said.

"I'm *comfortable* as a mess. I swear, if I dropped dead on the carpet right this minute, you'd tidy me up before the undertakers came."

"Goes without saying." She leaned up the stairs. "Naia, break open the champagne, he's off now!"

Up in her room Naia was trying to predict the courses of the gobs of snow on the glass. Close enough, most of the time. She left them to decide their own destinies and went out. On the landing she peered over the rail. Down in the hall, her dad was looking uncharacteristically smart. They waited for her to come down; then her father reached for her and the three of them headed for the front door side by side, him in the middle. He kept his arms around their shoulders all the way. Not like him at all. Mum was the demonstrative one.

"Now what's the procedure while I'm away?"

"Procedure?" they both said.

"With strangers at the door."

"Don't open it to them?" Alex hazarded innocently.

"Correct."

"How will we know if they're strangers unless we open the door?" This was Naia.

"Well, if you have to open the door, and they *are* strangers," he replied, "don't let them in."

"Why would we, if they're strangers?"

"They might want to read the meters."

"So if these strangers are meter readers"—Alex's turn—"we're not to let them read them?"

"What you do," he said patiently, "is ask for their IDs, and if they don't look genuine, you shut the door on them."

"How will we know if their IDs are genuine?"

"This is serious," Ivan said, realizing at last that he

was being set up. "The nearest neighbor is not only too far away to hear your screams, but stone deaf to boot."

They reached the end of the long hall. Ivan opened the front door. A gust of snow struck him full in the face.

"I could do without this. Just hope it's only local, that's all."

"No chance," Naia said cheerfully. "They said on last night's weather. Bad everywhere today, they said."

The wintry chill invaded the hall. Ivan flipped his coat collar up. Part of it stayed down. Alex moved to straighten it. He warned her off with a theatrically raised eyebrow.

"I'll give you a ring tonight," he said. "Midevening sometime, I expect."

"You'll be there before that," Naia said.

"I have to settle in."

"Go out on the town with your bit of stuff, you mean," Alex said.

"I'll tell her that's what you call her."

"She knows."

Ivan laughed and picked up the canvas holdall he'd dropped there earlier. He kissed them both on the forehead and stepped outside, walked to the garage, shoulders hunched against the whirling snow. Mother and daughter waited dutifully on the step, shivering a little, as he released the padlock, pulled the big wooden doors back, and went inside. In a minute they heard the engine turn over. Gravel crunched as the silver Saab reversed in a tight semicircle and aimed its nose at the drive. Ivan adjusted his coat and clipped his seat belt.

"Drive carefully!"

"Safe journey!"

Wheels churned. The stripped trees and bushes that lined the drive provided silver flashes of the car's departure all the way to the gate.

Alex plucked the two bottles of milk from the step. "I don't like the look of this snow," she said, straightening up.

"Oh, I do," said Naia.

"You don't have to drive all that way in it." Alex

shivered vigorously. "Remind me to go and shut the garage later."

"It could be half full of snow by then."

"Nothing stopping you doing it."

"Forget I spoke."

Alex kneed the door shut. "Any plans for the day? Studying, for instance?"

"Mother, the exams are almost three months away. I don't even want to *think* about them yet."

"It's never too early to start reviewing. You want to do well, don't you?"

"I will do well."

"Such confidence. But seeing as you're unoccupied, you can give me a hand around the house."

Naia's heart sank. "Oh, Mum," she said, following her to the kitchen.

Alex put the milk in the fridge. "I'll start upstairs, you get going down here. Big treat for you: You can use the new vacuum." She left the kitchen.

"Damn," Naia muttered. "Damn and sod and *blast*."

"And don't swear," a voice came back from the hall.

"Damn isn't swearing!" she shouted. "Bugger is swearing! Bastard is swearing! Bloody sodding hell is swearing!"

"Oh, that's all right then."

"And that's just for *starters*," she said, envisaging a mind-numbing morning cleaning the house when she could be doing nothing much. She'd been looking forward to doing nothing much.

7.3

It was known as the River Room because its French windows opened out onto the lawn that sloped gently down to the water's edge. This room was as far from the kitchen as it was possible to get without going upstairs, but so pleasant was it in summer that when his mother was alive they took most of their evening meals there from April to late October, reserving the actual dining room, with its serving hatch from the kitchen, for the darker months. But that was then. These days the room wasn't used at all, summer or winter, and with the door invariably closed it smelled stale and musty. Effectively sealed off from the minimalist comings and goings of Alaric and his father, with no heating and zero temperatures, it had also become one of the iciest rooms in the house.

When Alaric wandered in after his father's departure, it was with no real motive or intent. Perhaps, alone in the silent house, with the future so colorless, so void, his thoughts had turned to his mother. She often used to sit in the River Room on fine spring evenings and summer afternoons. She loved the smell of the water, the croaks and scuffles of the moorhens, the rustle and sway of the reeds and rushes. Sometimes she would sit at the open French windows, drawing. Several of her drawings were on the walls in thin black frames, alongside posters from unvisited exhibitions and international art shows.

The furniture was something of a hodgepodge: a plain 1920s dining suite, an Edwardian chaise lounge covered in faded blue velvet, a rosewood sideboard on which stood an assortment of family photographs—

Alaric at various stages of childhood, grandparents, Aunt Liney, a few other relatives, some of whom he hadn't seen for years, if ever. One of the photos, taken about ten years before, was of his mother on a beach in Pembrokeshire. She wore a black swimsuit and was nicely tanned. The ends of her short sandy hair were spiky with salt from a dip in the sea. She was trying to be serious for the camera, but her dancing eyes gave her away. It said so much about her, that picture. Outgoing, lively, quick to laugh. He picked up the photo. The sight of it had brought everything back in a rush; the good stuff first, then the rest, like a fist in the guts. He'd been trying not to put too much significance on the date, but he was making a poor job of it. His dad had forgotten without trying, but not him. How could he? Easier to forget Christmas or his own birthday.

Two years ago this very day, his mother had gone to see an Edvard Munch retrospective at the Tate Modern. It was early evening when she phoned from the train to say that it should reach the station in about twenty minutes. Ten minutes after her call, Dad had set off in the car to meet her. Alaric had been waiting for him to go so he could watch some of the sexy video he'd borrowed from Garth Noy. He ran up to his room, snatched it from his schoolbag, jumped down the stairs three at a time, and shoved the tape in the player. He was already well into the action when his father, having parked the car at the station, was going in to wait for the train, along with others who'd come to meet relatives or friends. They were still waiting fifteen minutes later, with growing puzzlement or irritation, when the announcement came over the speakers that the train from King's Cross had come off the tracks a couple of miles down the line. Casualties were feared. Later they were to learn that a single rail had been responsible for the accident. Already weakened by a "rolling contact fatigue crack," the freezing conditions of recent weeks had made the rail so brittle that when the wheels of this particular train on this particular night reached it, the section had shattered like glass into more than three hundred pieces. In spite of its enormous bulk and weight, the engine had shot up into the sky with a grinding roar, taking two of the passenger cars with it. Alaric's mother was in one of the cars. At the precise moment she was being catapulted through the train, Alaric, at home, was wondering if he had time for a trip to the bathroom. The reason he didn't make that trip was that he was too involved in the sweaty goings-on on the video. When his dad rang from the station, he had just freeze-framed an especially spicy scene. He snatched the phone somewhat distractedly. When he heard the news, his thumb twitched on the remote. The tape started again, sound effects and all.

"What's that?" Dad said. "Is there someone there? You all right, Al?"

Alaric ejected the video. "What do you mean, accident?"

"The train your mum rang from. I'm going down there. Can't just hang around here."

"I want to go, too!"

His father came back for him, then drove to the scene at reckless speed.

The derailed train resembled the corpse of a gigantic snake, slewing up into the night. A billowing pall of smoke and dust hung over everything as rescue teams smashed windows or tried to comfort those already released, who stood about in small shaken groups or sat alone, wrapped in blankets, watching. Relatives and other observers, Alaric and his father among them, were told to keep back while firemen sawed and hacked at the twisted cars. Arc lamps illuminated the scene, picking out every slow speck of falling dust while TV cameras recorded and reporters interviewed survivors for the viewers sitting comfortably at home. The night was laden with voices bellowing orders and shouting for assistance, the cries of young children and babies still inside the train, the angry snarl of electric saws, the thuds and crashes of massive hammers. Alaric had seen plenty of disasters and tragedies on television: motorway pileups, plane crashes (accidental or orchestrated), gutters running with the blood of murdered villains and innocents, the carnage created by suicide bombings, earthquakes that left ragged orphans howling through rubble for dead parents. He'd grown up with such images, contained within the boundaries of screens, and few had affected him much. Somebody else's world, somebody else's horror. Entertainment of a kind. But this was personal. In the extreme. Every now and then another passenger was freed or helped out. Some walked away, with or without assistance. A number were carried off on stretchers. The faces of a few on the stretchers were covered.

"Dad, that might be Mum under there!"

"We'll find out soon enough. Have to wait, it's all we can do."

"But Dad . . . "

"We have to *wait*, Al."

A priest was going around trying to comfort anxious relatives. Reaching Alaric and his father, he inquired if they had someone on the train.

"Wife and mother," Alaric's father snapped dismissively.

"They might not be among the . . . " the priest said

gently, unaware of the other's contempt for all churches, all faiths.

An angry glare fixed on him. "They? One person. My wife, my son's mother. And 'might not be among the' what? The dead? Is that the word you're searching for?"

The priest wilted with embarrassment. "I'll pray for her."

"Pray?" Alaric's father growled. "Who to? Look around you. Haven't you cottoned on yet, mate? There's no one at home up there."

She was brought out around two A.M. Her face was not covered, but her eyes were closed. When they spoke to her, she didn't hear. Nor did she show any sign of feeling them holding her hands in the ambulance. At the hospital, she was whisked away and they were left in a corridor, fretting helplessly, unable to look at each other. They weren't the only relatives waiting for news. One middle-aged couple had received theirs and clung together, sobbing quietly. After some time, Alaric's father went in search of information. When he returned, his face was ashen.

"It doesn't look good, Al. They're going to operate, but—I have to tell you this—they give her no more than a fifty-fifty chance."

A fifty-fifty chance. Fifty-fifty, fifty-fifty, the phrase had gone round and round in his head for the rest of the night. Afterward, when it was all over, it returned to haunt him, with the inescapable question: If those were the odds, why hadn't she pulled through? She'd had an even chance. She *might* have lived.

But she hadn't.

Pain, despair, month on month of empty, aching loneliness. Anger, too, because she'd left him without warning, without even saying good-bye. He felt abandoned and betrayed—and ashamed of himself for what he'd been up to at the time of the accident. A heady cocktail of bitterness, grief, and guilt. Everyone said it would get better, and they were right; it did. But while all else slowly dissolved, the loss and the absence never quite went away, were always there, coloring, shading, distorting everything.

There were tears in his eyes as he returned his mother's

photo to its place on the sideboard. The tears hindered his judgement, and the back of his hand nudged something. When he saw what it was, another memory rushed at him. Three and a half years ago. He was coming in from school, crossing the garden from the side gate. His mother saw him through the kitchen window and rushed out, tugged him excitedly inside, showed him the dusty object on the battered old refectory table.

"Look what I found in the attic!"

It was a bell-shaped glass dome, about a foot tall, on a round wooden base. It contained an elaborate arrangement of wax fruit, formless in parts, and faded from prolonged exposure to warmth and direct sunlight in earlier decades. He wasn't impressed.

"Do you know what it is?" she asked him.

He shrugged. "Bunch of moldy old fruit in a glass thingy."

"It's a Victorian shade. Maybe Edwardian, can't be sure, no expert."

"Shade?"

"That's what they called them. No respectable

parlor or drawing room was complete without one on the sideboard or mantelpiece or occasional table. You don't see many of them about these days. I've seen some lovely examples in museums, though."

"All full of ancient fruit?"

"Fruit, seashells, artificial flowers, dried ferns and grasses, stuffed birds, small animals."

"Yuck."

"Yes, I'd have given the dead wildlife a miss myself. But some of the others were quite tasteful. This one must have looked rather lovely in its day."

"Worth anything?"

"Not in this condition. I'd love to know if it was bought off the shelf or created by the lady of the house."

"Which lady, which house?"

Very carefully, his mother turned the shade over. On the base there was a small yellow-brown label, and faint handwriting. He could just make out ELVIRA UNDERWOOD, 1905.

"Never heard of her."

"She was the wife of Withern's original owner. He built the place in the 1880s, lived here till he died—in 1905."

"It can't have been in the attic all that time," Alaric said. "There were no Underwoods here for quite a few years."

"Sixteen," said his mother, who'd been researching Underwood family history. "Two possibilities. It was left in the attic by your great-gran when she sold in 1947, and the new owners didn't get around to chucking it; or it was put up there by Grandpa Rayner when he bought the place back in the 1960s."

"You're not thinking of putting it on show, are you?"

"I am!"

"But it's so . . . *ratty*."

"Well, the fruit's had it," she conceded. "But the glass and the base are still intact. Thought I'd make something of my own to put inside."

"What?"

"Don't know yet. Something."

Three and a half years later, he recalled the enthusiasm

with which she set to work on the project. He was used to her making things, but it wasn't until after her death that he realized how truly gifted his mother had been. She'd been able to turn her hand to so many things but had profited hardly at all from her numerous creations. Profit had been no more important to her than recognition of her talents. What little recognition there was had come from her students at the college, where she taught art part time: teenagers during the day, adults two evenings a week.

Construction of the new centerpiece for the old shade took much of her free time that autumn. She worked in secret, behind the closed door of her little studio (actually a wooden shed) next to the garage. All Alaric knew about the work in progress was that she was making something out of a lump of wood from the recently pruned oak in the south garden—the Family Tree, as it was known. Sometimes he saw her darting about outside, taking pictures of the house, but curious as he was, he could get nothing out of her. When the work was finished at last, she ushered him once again into the kitchen and stood him before the table. She had carefully draped a tea towel over the shade, and only when she was satisfied that he was ready and eager did she whip the cover off, with a dramatic cry of:

"Behold! Lexie's Folly!"

The jaded wax fruit arrangement had been replaced by a meticulously crafted wooden replica of their house. Faithful to the original in every noticeable detail, there was nothing remotely cute about the Withern Rise inside the glass dome. Wherever there was a chipped brick or broken drainpipe on the actual house, there was a chipped brick or broken drainpipe on the model. Even the gray slates on the three roofs, from which four tall chimneys rose, were individually etched and painted to look like the real slates. The main reference for the roof had been an aerial photo, taken five or six years earlier, that hung in the hall. Alaric noticed that one of the little chimneys was slightly skewed, as on the real roof, and there was even a crack in a small side window that corresponded with a crack in the south-facing storage-room window. As for the ivy, it was a virtual miracle. It was carved, of course, like all the rest, but it looked as alive as the real ivy that clung to the walls of the house itself.

"What did you call it?" he asked.

"Lexie's Folly."

"Folly?"

"A folly is a building or ruin of no practical use, built for fun, or on a whim, or to commemorate something." She sought his eye. "Do you like it?"

"It's incredible."

"Yes. I'm quite pleased with myself."

Lexie's Folly, or more often than not just "the Folly," was the term now used to describe the glass-domed shade. It was placed on the rosewood sideboard in the River Room, where Alaric soon got as used to it as to any other ornament and stopped gazing at it in wonder. Since his mother's death he'd hardly seen it at all, his visits to that room being so rare. He was only looking at it now because he had knocked it accidentally. But at once he was captivated all over again, marveling at the detail, the accuracy, the skill of the hand that had carved and colored it. Dusty as it was, the glass dome managed to reflect the snow falling across the windows of the room, and he found that if he squatted down and gazed at the little house with half-closed eyes, it was like looking at the real house in a snowstorm. His imagination put lights in the minuscule windows, warmth in the rooms behind them, and there grew in him an intense longing for the Withern Rise after which his mother had so painstakingly fashioned this exquisite replica. Withern as it was when she was with them. When they were a family.

At some point while his mind's eye wandered through the perfect little house, he had put his hands on the dome. When he felt a tingling in his palms, he thought nothing of it, but he couldn't ignore the excruciating pain that seared through him immediately afterward. His hands flew from the Folly, but the pain did not lessen with the severing of the contact. If anything it intensified, doubling him over. It lasted no more than fifteen or twenty seconds, but so acute was the agony that when it began to recede he remained hunched over, eyes tight shut, fearing its return. But then something touched his cheek. Something damp and very cold. He opened his eyes. Flakes of snow danced about his head like drunken fireflies. Snow? He stared about him, too numb to be astonished. He was standing on grass. Boughs and tangled branches filled his sky. He was in the south garden, under the Family Tree. What am I doing here? he thought. I should be indoors, in the River Room, not—

Walls, a ceiling, furniture formed about him. The tree, the grass, the garden vanished. He toppled backward with shock, onto the River Room floor. He sensed shapes, colors, odors that weren't quite right, but before he could investigate any of this he heard something that took his mind off all else: a voice just outside the door. And then the door was opening and someone was coming in. A girl of his own age, who squawked when she saw him, jumped back and stared at him with an expression of horror. An expression very much like his own.

7.4

Whatever Naia might have expected to find upon entering that room, it was not a teenage boy crouching on the floor. She fell back against the door, which promptly closed, stammering "Who . . . who?" and heard the same garbled inquiry from him. Trying hard to compose herself, she then demanded to know what he was doing in their house, and again heard him utter the same words, at the very same instant.

It was he who broke the copycat pattern, jumping to his feet and asking, very fiercely, what she was after. "Whatever it is, you broke into the wrong house. We haven't got a thing worth pinching."

"Broke into . . . ?" The color which had drained from Naia's cheeks, flooded back. Who was this boy? What was he talking about? She glanced at the French windows. They were closed and didn't look as if they'd been forced. "How did you get in, anyway?"

He didn't take his eyes off her. Didn't dare. She'd looked toward the French windows. Why? In the hope that he would look too, so she could bash him with something? Yes, that was it. There was something in the hand at her side, obviously a weapon of some sort.

"I'll give you one minute," he said, ignoring her question and trying to sound bolder than he felt. If you're still here after that, I'm picking up the phone."

There wasn't a phone in the River Room, but he had to say something with a threat in it. Sort of in the rules, situations like this. Unfortunately, the girl didn't seem intimidated.

"Pick up the phone? To call who, exactly?"

"The fairies at the bottom of the garden, who do you think?" he retorted angrily. Even as he said it, he wanted to kick himself until he begged for mercy. The fairies at the bottom of the *garden*?

Naia laughed. She couldn't help it. "Tell you what. You call the fairies, I'll call my mother, then we can all have a nice chat until the police get here."

The mention of the police—or her mother—clearly shocked him. He visibly wilted. Keen to capitalize on her advantage, Naia tossed aside the lethal vacuum-cleaner part she'd brought in with her and folded her arms, hoping he would take her for a force to be reckoned with. Straight talk now, straight talk.

"You don't deserve it," she said, "but I'm going to be generous. Slip out through those doors and I won't tell anyone you've been here. But stay, keep arguing with me, and I fetch my mum. That's the deal."

Oh, it was straight all right. Straight out of a lousy TV cop show. But it seemed to do the job. The boy was looking even more bemused now—or worried, hard to tell which. His silence gave her a chance to look him over, and it was then that she saw what should have been unmissable from the start: that the things on his feet were more like slippers than shoes, and that he wasn't wearing anything over his sweater.

"Where's your coat?" she asked. "You can't have come out without a coat, weather like this." She looked around. No sign. "Did you take it off in another room? Which room? Have you already turned that one over?"

He might or might not have attempted some sort of explanation had a floorboard not creaked overhead. He jumped as though slapped.

"What's that?"

"My mum," Naia said. "Didn't believe me, did you? Thought I was alone here."

"What's your mum doing upstairs?"

"Oh, you know, the usual. Cleaning up after my dad, putting stuff down the loo, making the beds . . . "

"Making the beds? She's got no right to make the beds."

"No right? She'll love that. Hang on, I'll give her a shout, you can tell her in person."

She opened the door and was about to lean out when he leaped at her and spun her away. He slammed the door and positioned himself between it and her, blocking any further move in that direction. He was wild eyed, agitated, potentially dangerous. She knew this, but had no intention of showing any weakness to scum like him.

"Not too keen on meeting my mother, are you?"

"All I want is for you to *go*," he said earnestly. "There's nothing here for you. We might have a big house, but we're not rich or anything."

It was Naia's turn to be puzzled. He seemed as if he really *believed* what he was saying. "I just don't understand what you're up to," she said. "I mean, what's going on here?"

"You tell me," he countered.

"What's your name?"

"My name? What's it to you?"

"It's nothing to me. I'm trying to give you a break, that's all."

"Okay, I'll tell you my name. It's Alaric Underwood, and my dad's only gone to the village. He'll be back any minute, then you'll be in trouble."

Naia frowned. "Underwood?"

"Oh, heard it before, have we?"

"You could say that. I've had enough of this. If you've been put up to this by some so-called friend, you're wasting your . . . " She stopped. He was staring from her face to something over her shoulder. "Now what?"

He didn't answer. Didn't seem capable. She glanced behind her. The mirror on the wall. He was comparing his reflected image with her unreflected one. She leaned sideways to try and see what so amazed him, and caught half of her face next to his. She pulled back for a better view, better perspective—and gasped.

"You'd think we were related." She turned back to the boy. "You said your name's Underwood. You were kidding, right?"

"Why would I kid about my name?"

"Because it's my name, too. But you knew that, must have. You've got some scam going here."

"You're crazy."

"One of us is."

She leaned forward and gripped his chin. He jerked his head away. She reached again. This time he let her. She tilted his jaw to view his face from various angles.

"Same eyes," she said. "Same nose, ears, jaw, hair color, everything."

He was about to respond when a drawer closed noisily in the room above. His eyes flew to the ceiling like startled birds. Now some item of furniture was being dragged up there. Feeling suddenly trapped and outnumbered, he groped behind him for support. Finding none, he turned to look.

"Where's the table? The chairs?"

"We got rid of them," Naia said.

"Got . . . what?"

"New dining suite coming. You mean you didn't know?" She smirked. "But I thought this was *your* house."

He stared about him for the first time. Literally the first time. The faded blue covering of the chaise had been replaced by a lush red velvet. The curtains were of similar material, very unlike the old beige ones that should be hanging there. There was a new carpet and lamp, and a vase of flowers on the windowsill. The rosewood sideboard was still in place, but it was a long time since he'd seen it gleaming like that. There were photos on it, some of which he didn't recognize, along with several new ornaments, and—highly polished for a change—the old shade: his mother's Folly. How could he have failed to notice these things? He hadn't even questioned the warmth of the room!

His eyes darted about, trying to take in everything at once. There were pictures on the walls that he knew and pictures that he did not. Among the latter was a group of black-and-white photographs of New York skyscrapers, desert sandscapes, gnarled and twisted trees. On another wall there hung a larger black-and-white, in which a young woman, naked, was bending over a freestanding washbasin next to a window with a crude splintered shutter. A water pitcher and a mortar and pestle stood on the uneven flagstone floor. The picture was titled *Le Nu Provençal,* attributed to French photographer Willy Ronis, and Alaric knew it very well, remembered every detail, especially of the girl at the basin: the light from the window splashing her shoulders, the contours of her calves and buttocks, the hint of profiled breast. The date on the photo, 1949, had struck him almost as much as the girl herself when he first saw it, because he couldn't take his eyes off her even when he realized that she must have been born some years before either of his grandmothers, and would now be getting on for eighty. His mother had bought the print a couple of months before she died. She'd been looking for just the right frame for it; hadn't managed to find it. But here it was, on the wall, framed.

Alaric whirled around. "This isn't my house!"

Naia clapped her hands lightly. "At last!"

He turned his back on her. She didn't exist. He wouldn't let her. None of this existed. He sought something familiar; found it on the sideboard. He rushed at the Folly, placed his hands around the dome, closed his eyes to shut out this bright false room. This time there was no pain. Somewhere behind him the girl was lobbing questions at him, but he found her easy to ignore with his back to her. And then she fell silent, and the air became very cold, and there was nothing between his hands. He opened his eyes. He was in the south garden again, under the tree. Good. But it wasn't enough. "Not *here*!" he shouted. A small pause, then four walls, a floor, and a ceiling formed about him, and familiar furniture in a familiar condition. The Folly on the dusty sideboard was the first thing he saw as the chill loneliness of the real River Room enveloped him. He sank to his knees in abject relief.

7.5

He was in the kitchen, looking for something to drink, when the doorbell rang. Liney. The last person he needed right now. Apart from the fact that he had rather a lot to think about all of a sudden, once he let her in she would take over the house and his life until Dad came home with Kate, curse her, whereupon *she* would impose *herself* instead. It was tempting to avoid setting phase one of this dismal future in motion by pretending he was out and hoping she would turn around and drive back home. The reason he didn't was that there wasn't a rat in hell's chance of her doing any such thing. The loopy old bat would either camp out on the step until someone turned up, or break in.

The first thing she said when he opened the door to her and she came in was, "My god, haven't you people heard of *heating*?" He informed her that the boiler was kaput. "You're pulling my leg," she said.

He denied this. "You mean . . . there's no hot water?"

"No, there's hot water. Just no heat."

"*Just* no heat! Doesn't your misbegotten father know it's the middle of February and *snowing*?"

"He probably does."

The afternoon found him on the old leather footstool in the Long Room, the thousand pieces of a jigsaw spread across the big coffee table before him. "I thought you'd like it," Liney had said when she handed him The Paradoxes and Illusions of M. C. Escher. "You did?" he replied incredulously, thinking, You're even crazier than I thought. But he'd felt obliged to start the puzzle because even though he'd known his aunt all his life, he still felt rather overwhelmed by her. Every now and then, as he hunched over it, she would appear at his side like an unwanted genie and pounce on a piece he might or might not have been looking for, then drop it into place. One more irritation to chalk up against her.

Few would have guessed to look at them that Alaric's mother and his aunt were sisters. While his mother had been of medium height, compact, with short fair hair and blue eyes, Liney was tall and angular, with eyes like green gobstoppers. Her frizzy reddish hair stood up like a badly cut hedge, giving her a perennially startled look. Alaric had said more than once that she looked like a witch. He didn't know it, but Liney had an even better one. She liked to say that her sister had taken after their mother while she had taken after the dog.

The Escher jigsaw wasn't the only thing that kept Alaric in the Long Room. Liney had discovered a four-bar electric heater in one of the cupboards under the stairs, taken off the plug when it refused to work, fiddled with the wires, and plugged it in with her eyes shut in case she'd muddled them up. Shortly, to her delight, the dust on the old elements was sizzling nicely. Then, a faint glow, gradually becoming more livid, and Liney jumping up and down like a hot-wired grasshopper. Alaric refused to show or express pleasure but did not reject the small warmth. A cozy scene, potentially: crouching over a jigsaw and a small electric fire while snow walloped the windows and steadily transformed the garden into a different land; but it was wasted on him. His mind was in a loop that started and ended with the morning's adventure. He had quickly ditched the easy notion that he must have blacked out or fallen into some sort of stupor and dreamed it. The other River Room and the girl who seemed so at home there were not imaginative constructs of his unconscious. He knew this with absolute certainty but could take it no further. The Paradoxes and Illusions of M. C. Escher was a doddle by comparison.

7.6

It defied logic. Things like that didn't happen. But she'd seen it with her own eyes, and Naia Underwood had too much respect for her senses to mistrust the evidence they presented her with. Even at school she was becoming known for her imagination, her inquiring mind. "A physicist in the making," Mrs. Petrie, her science teacher, had said at the last parents' evening.

With very little ado, she was able to take the morning's encounter at face value and move on to wondering who the boy was and where he'd come from and returned to. She recalled his horror upon realizing that he wasn't where he'd believed himself to be, the way he'd run to the Folly as if to some powerful talisman or instrument of salvation. She'd watched dumbfounded as he faded to nothing, shivering at the sudden drop in temperature. Then everything was as it should have been once again, even the Folly. You would have thought, from the way he'd been gripping it, that the Folly would have gone with him, but when he vanished it remained in its place on the sideboard.

During the hours that followed, Naia came up with several theories about what had occurred and who the boy was, but one by one she discarded them as being unfeasible or too fanciful by half, until only a couple continued to seem worthy of consideration. She considered them.

7.7

When Alaric was little and Aunt Liney had visited, she used to reach for him and clutch him to her and cover his face with big sloppy kisses. He would wriggle out of her arms in terror, and she would howl with laughter. It was at least three years since she had last covered him with kisses. One of the few perks of being a teenager, he decided.

Liney had cooked the tea and washed up afterward. The meal was horrible, the washing-up inept. He could have done a better job of both, but kept this to himself. He didn't want her there, so she could damn well pay for inconveniencing him. Liney wasn't easy to relax with, forever jumping up and fiddling with things that were perfectly all right as they were. This inability to sit still for long was one of the few things she had in common with his mother, but it did not endear her to him. She'd been unusually still for the better part of an hour, though, sitting sideways on the couch with her feet up. Her feet in those wrinkly socks of hers looked enormous. The socks were but a sample of Liney's extensive wardrobe of homemade garments, almost all of which were too big, too bright, and shapeless. She had a flat in Sheringham on the north Norfolk coast, above her own craft shop. In the shop she sold other people's work, some of it very fine, while her flat was crammed with her own wonky lampshades, crudely glazed pots, garish watercolors, and great clunky bits of jewelry.

While Alaric bowed his head over the Escher jigsaw, Liney, on the couch, knitted. The needles she used were so long that she had to sit with her head thrown back in order to keep her eyes focused. What she was knitting—a dazzling construction of peculiar dimensions and form—was a mystery to him, as it might have been to her. While she worked, she contributed to a TV quiz show, shouting things like "General theory of relativity!" and "Napoleon!" to questions whose answers turned out to be "The hanging gardens of Babylon" and "Freddie Mercury." Television was a novelty to Liney. She didn't possess one herself and claimed not to want one, but she seemed to be enjoying the quiz, in her way. She had no trouble wrenching her attention away from it, however, when the phone in the hall rang. Simultaneously throwing her knitting in the air and trampolining off the couch in order to flee the room, she snatched up the receiver before it was halfway through the third ring.

"Hello? Ivan! Hi, how ya doing, boy?"

After a spot of inconsequential chat, she called Alaric to the phone.

"Hello."

"Al! I'm ringing from Newcastle!" He made it sound as if he'd reached the North Pole after weeks of hardship, a diet of husky and ice, with gangrenous toes. "Liney tells me it's snowing pretty hard there. Seems to have followed me. Coming down like nobody's business here."

"Really."

The conversation continued in this stilted fashion for a minute or two before fizzling out completely, and it was with some relief that Alaric returned to the Long Room, where he found his aunt stabbing at the TV remote in a vain attempt to avoid the news, which seemed to have just come on every channel. The contents of her own head were bad enough news, she always said, without the rest of the world's problems.

"Anything to report?" she asked, glaring at the screen.

"Report?"

"From Newcastle."

He returned to his puzzle. "Snowing there."

"That all?"

"Just about."

Liney hit the off button. Silence rattled down like the blade of a guillotine. Minutes passed. About as good at silence as at most other things, Liney, clutching at conversational straws, asked Alaric how he was doing at school. He told her that he was doing okay, mainly because the truth would lead to more questions. The blade fell again. Liney tried whistling through her teeth, but finding that she couldn't whistle badly and knit badly at the same time, gave up the whistling. Eventually . . .

"I was thinking of making some hot chocolate. Fancy some?"

This was the first thing she'd said since her arrival that had the slightest interest for him. Liney's hot chocolate was a concoction of her own devising that, to the amazement of everyone who knew her and tried it, worked brilliantly. The ingredients (carried with her whenever she went away) were Belgian cocoa, chicory and coffee extract, dark muscovado cane sugar, and brandy, all whisked up by hand in skimmed milk while warming slowly on the burner.

Postchocolate, good-nights said, Alaric lay in bed listening to his aunt banging about downstairs. Soon she came up. He knew the house so well that he could tell which stair she was on by its individual creak. He heard her go into the bathroom at the top of the stairs. Then the water pipes were thumping, the way they did when the hot tap was run too fast.

Five minutes later she emerged, and after a pause closed the guest-room door with a small but decisive click. Ordinary everyday sounds, every one, but how different even a door can sound when closed by someone you don't know well. It would be like that when Kate Faraday came, he thought. Everything she did would be unfamiliar and consequently irritating. Kate had visited them for a week last September, sleeping in the room Liney was using now. He hadn't minded her then; rather liked her, in fact. She had a good sense of humor, and she was warm and open. But that was before she had decided to move in with them. Now he minded her very much.

Even though it was midwinter and late and his light was off, it wasn't completely dark in Alaric's room. He'd pulled the curtains back to watch the snow fall while he lay in bed. By morning it would cover everything beyond the window.

Ordinarily he might have looked forward to seeing the new white world the day would bring, but even after all these hours he was unable to think of anything else but the girl who looked so much like him and claimed to share his name. She even had a River

Room, and an old glass shade with a perfect Withern
Rise inside. If nothing else was impossible, this was.
His mother had made only one Folly. There could *be*
no other. So the whole thing was impossible.

Wasn't it?

7.8

Naia dreamed.

In the dream she was an observer, watching a young
boy climb the Family Tree in the south garden. There
was something about him that reminded her of the
morning's unexpected visitor, though the boy in the
dream was younger: ten, eleven, twelve at a push.
Having already climbed higher than was sensible, he
crawled out along a branch. It was summer, the tree
was in full leaf, and she couldn't see him very well.
Suddenly there was a crack. The boy fell. It was a long
drop. He hit the ground hard and didn't get up. Naia
knew that he was dead.

But then, as is the way with dreams, something odd
happened. The body on the ground became two, lying

side by side, identical in every respect except that the second boy got to his feet and climbed back up the tree. Then a great slow rolling tide of water covered the garden and the body on the ground. Naia woke abruptly to find her sheets soaking wet. She was horrified. She couldn't remember the last time this had happened. She cleaned up after herself as quietly as she could, so as not to wake her mother, and climbed back in.

After a little tossing and turning she again slept, and again dreamed—the same dream, but for one small difference. As before, it was summer. As before, the boy climbed the tree, and after going out too far fell to his death. Again, a short pause; then the one body divided and became two, and the first remained quite still while the second stood up. But this time the living boy did not climb the tree. He walked away.

And the garden remained unflooded, her bed dry.

Day Six

6.1

It was freezing when he woke. His breath hovered above him like small blue pockets of fate. His bedside clock told him it was past ten. Well, school vacation, stay there all day if he wanted. But he didn't want. Too damn cold, for one thing. Not that it would be much warmer out of bed, zero heating and all. Still, he crawled out and shrugged his winter bathrobe on. It was too small for him now; his wrists protruded from the sleeves like cuffs. He went downstairs. He knew where Liney was well before he got to the kitchen by her screechy duet with Bryan

Adams. "Mor-ning," she sang as he entered.

"Morning," he said, and turned the radio down.

"I haven't made any breakfast. Wasn't sure what you have." He drew back the larder door and rattled a cereal box at her. "I've arranged for someone to come and look at the heating," she said.

"Just look at it?"

"Hopefully fix it."

"When?"

"Tomorrow morning, early."

He tipped the cereal into a bowl. "Dad know?"

"No. Be a surprise for him."

"Like the bill, when it arrives."

"By then he'll be too warm to care."

He shoveled his cereal down without ceremony and went upstairs again. While he got dressed, he put on a CD. He left it on repeat to give the impression that he was still there when he went back down. Liney was still in the kitchen, air-miking "Better Be Good to Me" with Tina Turner. From the foot of the stairs he crossed the hall, entered the River Room, and closed the door.

It felt even colder in there than yesterday. He plunged his hands into his armpits and stood at the French windows. Snow had fallen steadily throughout the night, was falling still. The garden was white and flawless, the snow-laden trees across the river works of art. But he hadn't come in here to look at the view. He turned to the domed ornament on the sideboard. Overnight he'd become certain that the Folly was the key. He'd been touching it just before opening his eyes in the garden yesterday. It hadn't been with him outside, but there'd been an exact copy of it in the other River Room, and his hands had been on that one, too, seconds before his return.

He wiped some of the dust off with his handkerchief. The snow filling the windows of the room immediately found a purer reflection in the curved glass. He gazed down at the little house and thought of the woman who'd carved it. The model was as like the real house as any replica could be, but it was the Withern Rise his mother had known, cared for, made her own; not the one he and his father had let go.

Filled suddenly with a yearning to be at the house of better days, Alaric put his hands on the dome. He'd been planning this since waking. Planning the impossible: a miracle from a homemade wooden object under glass. It wasn't plugged in to anything, nothing powered it, but something had happened yesterday, and the ornament he knew as Lexie's Folly had made it happen.

When he felt a tingling in his palms, his heart leaped. The tingling wasn't unpleasant, but the next part was, and it was all he could do not to cry out when the pain slithered like a host of eager snakes through veins and arteries and into his chest and every other part of him. He staggered, agonized, only just managed to keep his eyes open. He wanted to witness every step and stage of this. What he saw through the veil of pain was the room wavering like a flimsy stage set, becoming translucent, and the old tree rearing up, its great boughs and numberless branches unfurling like cables and strings overhead. Then he saw, lower down, farther off, the garden slotting itself into place, piece by piece by piece, like an automated version of Liney's jigsaw. When the garden was complete, the last of the room faded away, taking the debilitating pain with it, and Alaric lay gasping on cold white grass.

The snow, covering exposed roots and a fallen bough that had yet to be disposed of, fell like a white bead curtain at the tree's rim; but it was not impenetrable. Alaric sat up and peered. Everything looked exactly as it should in such conditions: house, trees, bushes, the old garden wall, the garage . . .

The garage! Shouldn't the doors be green? They had been last time he looked. But these doors had been stripped back to the wood. The main door of the house, too. And the front step was clear of all the boxes and bags of rubbish that Dad had been piling there for weeks. And then there was the ivy. It should be scrambling unchecked across the walls all the way to the roof, so thick in places that its own weight threatened to pull it away. This ivy was neat, controlled, trimmed right back.

He got to his feet. So. It wasn't his house, his garden.

The tree he sheltered under was not his Family Tree. None of this was his or his family's. Not a thing.

6.2

Naia had spent much of the morning in her room, partly to avoid the household tasks her mother would have inflicted on her at sight, partly because she expected yesterday's visitor to return. How could he not, now that he knew about her? She tried closing her eyes with one of her mother's "relaxing" tapes on in the background, but this just made her drowsy. She didn't want to be drowsy, she wanted to be alert for when he came. If he came.

She turned off the tape, went back to *The Catcher in the Rye*.

6.3

He cursed his stupidity. He'd willfully engineered this return, known that if he succeeded he would find himself outside first of all; but he hadn't had the wit to dress for the weather. He was even wearing slippers again. Slippers in the snow! No wonder he was crap at school. He looked at the house. It might not be his, but he had to get inside if he didn't want to freeze to death. He'd gotten in easily enough yesterday. Effortlessly, without trying. How had he done that? He stood shivering, helpless, thinking of the warmth to be had inside, at such a loss as to how to get to it that he felt little surprise, only relief, when four walls rose about him, a ceiling formed above him, a carpeted floor rolled out beneath him. And . . .

"Took you long enough. I was starting to think you'd never come. But did you *have* to bring all that snow in?"

6.4

She sat on the floor, leaning against the bed, her knees acting as a book rest. To look at her, so relaxed, so casual, you'd think he had come in through the door, by arrangement, instead of out of nowhere in a whirl of snowflakes. He stared about him, skin burning with the rush of warmth.

"My room! Why am I up here?"

"Because I brought the Folly up last night." She indicated it on the bookcase. "I wasn't certain till now, but just before you appeared it went all peculiar, like there was more than one of it, or I was seeing double. I imagine it was gearing up to receive you or whatever. I'm right in guessing that you've got a Folly, too?"

"Yes . . ."

"There you are then. Yours sends you off, mine pulls you in. Look, you're ruining my carpet. Take off your slippers, will you? Why are you wearing slippers anyway if you've been outside? Come to that, *why* have you been outside? Hang on, I'll find some paper."

She tossed her book aside and dived under the bed as if it was what everybody did after greeting someone. While she was down there, Alaric took in his surroundings. It was his room all right, and he knew a number of the things in it intimately: the old easy chair, the chest of drawers, the corner cupboard and wardrobe, the bookcase (though there were more books on this one). The things he did not recognize were new, feminine, or furnishings that would not have been his choice.

"Put them on this."

He took off his slippers and placed them on the Christmas wrapping paper Naia unrolled. He felt disconcertingly vulnerable without footwear of any kind.

"It's all right," Naia said, catching his nervous glance at the door. "There's only Mum and me, and she's downstairs. I always hear her coming if there's no music on."

"What if she does come?"

She seated herself on the bed. "You'll have to skedaddle, sharpish."

"What do you suggest, I jump out the window?"

"You use the Folly."

"It's not that easy. It needs . . . preparation."

"You managed without much preparation last time."

He flung himself into the easy chair and leaned

back, experiencing the familiarity of it. It was his chair in every respect. There was even a loose spring in the seat that dug into your backside. He felt something under his palm, where it fell on one of the armrests. He tilted his hand; found a rip in the material exactly like the one he'd made when he dropped a pair of scissors in that very place when he was ten or eleven. This detail startled him as much as anything he'd seen or heard so far. Could it be that this girl had dropped scissors there when *she* was ten or eleven?

"What is it?"

He covered the rip with his hand. "Nothing."

From deep in the old chair, he searched out more differences. Most were very obvious. The walls, for instance, were papered: a delicate purple and green pattern. The walls of his room were painted: black and red, his favorite colors when he was thirteen. His curtains were pale blue, in need of a wash; hers matched her wallpaper and looked fresh. On her window ledge there were dolls and stuffed animals and ornaments she'd outgrown but didn't want to part with. Mostly there was just litter and dust on his ledge. He'd dumped most of his old stuff ages ago, including his Action Men, his miniature car collection, almost two hundred Beanos. His once-prized collection of Marvel and DC Comics were stacked in the storage room.

Everywhere you looked above head height in this room there were wind chimes, slowly revolving mobiles—butterflies, stars, little parasols—and dream catchers that Naia had made herself, using yarn and feathers and other materials. Nothing dangled from Alaric's ceiling but the odd spider or cobweb.

Naia was watching him. "Is it very like yours," she said, "or just fairly?"

"I'm a bit short of dolls."

He stood up suddenly and headed for the door.

"Where are you going?"

"Want to see what else is the same."

"Don't! Mum might see you."

"You said she was downstairs."

"For now, yes, but—"

"And you said you'd hear her."

He opened the door a crack and peered out at a familiar galleried landing. At the far end of the landing, near the bathroom, a stairway began its long descent. Halfway down, at a platform a yard square, the stairs turned at a right angle, as did the lofty wall, and continued on to the hall below. He knew without counting that there were twenty-six steps, thirteen per flight.

The painted sections of the half-paneled walls, on which hung a great many pictures of various types and sizes, were a crisp yet muted yellow. The walls below the landing of his own house were pale green, as they had been for years.

"Well?" Naia said as he closed the door.

"The same."

"You mean like in a mirror?"

"No, not like in a mirror," he said irritably. "Nothing's back to front. What do you think this is, Alice through the frigging looking glass?"

"No need to bite my head off."

"Well."

"Yesterday was the first time you came here, wasn't it?"

"Yeah. Didn't know you existed till then." He glanced about. "You or this."

"What do you have to do?"

"Do?"

"To make the Folly work."

He shrugged. "Complicated."

"Complicated, or you just don't want to let me in on it?"

"Take your pick."

"You know, I might have thought you were a ghost, the way you disappeared yesterday," Naia said. "If I believed in ghosts. Which I don't."

"Tell me what you saw."

"I saw you disappear."

He scowled. "*Describe* it."

"Well, the room went sort of unreal, then you went unreal, too, then you kind of . . . dissolved. I ought to video it another time, so you can see for yourself."

"What do you call this place?"

"I call it my room."

"The house," he snapped.

"Withern Rise. Withern for short."

"Guess what mine's called."

She didn't need to. "What about outside?"

"Outside?"

"Is it the same, too? The garden and all."

He leaned over the bed, looked out of the window at the river.

"I've had this view all my life."

"Takes some believing," she said.

"Don't start that again."

"Well, you have to admit . . . "

He straightened up. "Yeah."

"What did you say your name was? Alec? Eric?"

"Alaric."

He'd never cared for his name. The number of times it had been called for one reason or another and heads had turned to see who it belonged to. Fortunately his friends usually abbreviated it. Dad, too, most of the time. Mum hardly ever had. He hadn't minded it coming from her so much.

"I've heard that name before somewhere," Naia said.

"It was my great-grandfather's."

"That's it. My great-grandpa's, too."

Alaric returned to the chair. "What's yours?"

"Naia. After my gran, Granny Bell. Her middle name."

"I had a Granny Bell, too. Don't think I ever knew her middle name."

"While we're on names," Naia said, "what are your parents called?"

"My dad's name is Ivan."

"Ivan Underwood?"

"Of course Ivan Underwood."

"Ditto. They couldn't be brothers, could they? Secret brothers, unknown to each other, separated at birth?"

He sneered. "With the same first *and* last name?"

"Have you got a picture?"

"What of?"

"Your father, bonehead."

"Oh, sure, I always carry a picture of my old man."

"Tell me what he looks like then."

"He's my father, I don't spend a lot of time looking at him."

"So if he was in a room full of strangers, or a police lineup, you wouldn't be able to pick him out?"

"He's about so high," Alaric said. "Not fat but getting a bit of a gut . . . " He floundered.

"Eyes?" Naia said.

"Yeah, he's got a couple of those."

"Color."

"Sort of greeny gray, I think."

"Hair getting a bit thin on top?"

"Mmm. He doesn't like to talk about it. Got some gray at the sides, doesn't mind that."

"Thinks it makes him look distinguished," Naia said.

"Right."

"What does he do for a living?"

"Got a shop in Stone. Yours?"

"Shop in Stone. Does it have a name?"

"Underwood's Antiques," he said.

"And Memorabilia?"

"And Memorabilia."

"My dad's gone to the collectors' fair in Bristol. Annual event. Yours there, too?"

"No. Gave Bristol a miss this year. Something much more interesting on. In Newcastle."

"What's in Newcastle that beats the Bristol Collectors' Fair?"

"Kate Faraday."

Naia's face lit up. "You've even got a Kate Faraday?"

"Oh, yes."

She caught his tone. "Don't you like her?" He gave a telling grunt of contempt. "But Kate's lovely."

"Oh, *lovely*," he said.

"Wait a sec. Your dad's gone to Newcastle to see Kate? Specially to see her? Mine's never done that. They sometimes meet at the trade fairs because they're both in the same line of business, but that's all. Mum used to rib Dad something awful about her. 'Seeing the girlfriend, are we?' she'd say. In the end he said that if she thought there was something going on between them, he'd stop going to the fairs altogether."

"Decent of him."

"Mum told him not to be so daft and got him to invite her down after one of them."

"Kate came here?"

"September. For the weekend. Then again just before Christmas. They really get along, her and Mum. Write to each other all the time. All right, we've done our dads and Kates. Mums now. I've got a photo here." She shot off the bed and grabbed a large blue-and-green bag, which she proceeded to sift through on the floor. "So your dad's bringing Kate back to stay, is he?"

"Yes."

"Good of him to go all that way for her."

"She probably has a lot of stuff."

"A suitcase? A bag or two? Could have done it by train."

"She's not just coming to visit," he said.

Naia tugged a small plastic wallet out of the bag. "No? What then?"

"She's moving in."

She looked up. "Moving in? What, as a lodger? Brilliant!"

"With Dad. Into his room."

"Sleeping with him, eh?" She laughed at the absurdity of it.

"Well, she won't be sleeping on the *floor*," he said bitterly.

Naia rocked back on her haunches, still amused. "I bet your mum'd have something to say about that."

He reached out and took the wallet from her. Flipped it open. It contained two small transparent pockets. In one there was a color photo of Naia's father, in the other a picture of her mother.

"Was your mum . . . " He started again. "Was your mum in an accident?"

"Accident?"

"Railway accident. Train crash. Couple of years ago."

"Well, yes . . . "

She didn't think about it much these days. Didn't want to. That terrible night. The call from Dad at the station while she was watching a video borrowed from Kirsty Rowan. She'd insisted that he come back for her, and they'd spent hours beside the track, watching people being released and brought out. Then the dash to the hospital in the ambulance, and Dad pacing up and down, and going off in search of an update; coming back very serious and pale.

"It doesn't look good, Nai. They're going to operate, but—I have to tell you this—they give her no more than a fifty-fifty chance."

Fifty-fifty. Fifty-fifty. The phrase had gone round and round in her head for what seemed like hours. Would she pull through? Could she? Every time a doctor or nurse approached, her heart stopped. Was this it? The news she'd been dreading? She shuddered at the thought of what might have happened.

"She was lucky," she said.

"Lucky?"

"Could have died. Six did. She had an even chance. Touch and go."

He returned to the picture in the wallet. "Seven died in my mother's accident."

Naia started. "Seven?"

"When were these taken?"

"Last summer. Cornwall. Mum likes Cornwall."

"And your mother's name is . . . ?"

"Alexandra. Alex. Calls herself Lexie sometimes."

He held the wallet up before her. "My parents." Laid a finger against one of the photos. "My mother. Taken over a year after she died."

He tossed the wallet to Naia. She was too slow and missed it. It lay open in the space between them. Alaric got up and went to the window overlooking the south garden. Naia took advantage of his turned back and put the wallet hastily away, like evidence of a crime. Then, desperate to block out the unthinkable, she began prattling about how things had been for them after the accident, about her mum's headaches and the pains in her chest that had taken so long to go away, about how Dad had spent as much time as he could away from the shop, fussing around her, doing every-thing for her as if realizing what he'd so nearly lost.

"She wasn't herself for ages," Naia said. "Very down, very negative. There was none of the old sparkle. Dad took her out quite a bit—both of us—to try and jolly her along, give her new things to look at and think about. You should see our photo album, all the places we went to . . . "

A shutter had come down in Alaric's mind. He had his own memories of that year, and no photos.

"I can show you where she's buried," he said. Naia stopped talking. "The cemetery over the wall. There's a headstone with her name on it."

It was all she could do not to clap her hands over her ears. But it was too late. She'd heard it. It was in her head. Imprinted.

Alaric turned from the window and once again took in the room that was his, yet not. The day his mother died, the home she'd made for the three of them had begun to die, too. Colors had quickly dulled, as though switched off; cleaning and polishing had become a thing of the past; nothing was ever painted, repaired, tidied up; flowers had ceased to cross the threshold. Before long his father had put away most of the ornaments and bric-a-brac she'd collected over the years, reducing the number of reminders of her. Naia's house, what he'd seen of it, still boasted all the things that his had lost, and much more.

"Naia!"

They both went rigid at the sound of the voice, for different reasons. Naia bounded to the door, hurtled out, leaned over the banister.

"Where did all the bread go?" her mother asked from the foot of the stairs.

"I put it out for the birds like you told me to."

"I didn't mean *all* of it. There was almost a whole loaf there."

"Well, you said you were going to be baking."

"Yes, but not for the *birds*, child!"

A disgruntled Alex Underwood returned to her kitchen, and Naia went back to her room. She closed the door. Alaric was gone. His slippers were still on the Christmas wrapping paper.

6.5

All the way back—bedroom to garden to River Room—Alaric's head rang with that voice. *Her* voice. It was still with him as he sat down on the old chaise lounge and stared hopelessly about him. If his mother had lived, this room, and other rooms and parts of the house, would have been redecorated recently. A new dining suite would be on the way. There would be new pictures on the walls, new carpets and curtains. Anything that could be polished would have been polished, the windows would be clean, floors swept, carpets vacuumed. The heating would have been fixed, too. She wouldn't have put up with this cold for a minute.

But that wasn't the way of it. Not here. Not for him.

As the unfairness of all this stumbled around his mind, a lump rose in his throat and a sob escaped him that could not have been more badly timed. "Oh, there you are," Liney said, looking around the door. "I thought you were ups . . . Alaric? What's up? What's the matter?"

He swiped furiously at his cheeks, but she was already striding toward him, arms outstretched, then slapping his head against her bony chest like a bundle of washing. He didn't pull away, resist, do anything at all. His arms hung at his sides while he gulped more sobs, one after the other, like a big kid, unable to stop.

"What is it, love?" She'd never called him love before. Didn't sound right coming from her. "What is it, what is it?" She soothed him energetically, but stopped suddenly. "Alaric. There's snow on the carpet."

She released him, unable to stare at floors and hug simultaneously. There was more snow on his socks than the floor, but she hadn't noticed his feet yet. All other considerations paled alongside the problem of how to explain this. What reason could he possibly give for snow on his socks? She saw them. Her jaw dropped. Here it comes, he thought. But it didn't come. He was saved from interrogation by an unusual quirk in his aunt's intelligence. If something puzzled Liney and a solution didn't present itself in pretty short order, she didn't worry about it or niggle away at it; she turned her back on it and carried on as if it didn't exist or was perfectly normal. A simple philosophy that had served her very well over the years.

"I'd take them off if I were you," she said. "You don't

want chilblains. I know all about chilblains. Real martyr to chilblains, me."

While he removed his socks, Liney did a lightning sweep of the room to try and establish what might have caused his distress (the snow-on-socks puzzle having already been dismissed) and saw a picture on the sideboard, a photo of her sister that looked like it had been moved recently. All was immediately clear.

"What do I do with them?"

"Give 'em here, I'll put them in the wash."

She took the damp socks from him and draped them over the door handle to collect on her way out, which he knew wasn't going to be right away when she looped her thumbs in the back pockets of her baggy dungarees and turned to the window.

"I love the snow, don't you?" she said. "Always have. Your mum loved it, too. All that traipsing about in big boots and scarves and mittens. Rolling snowballs along the pavement till they were so massive you couldn't push them any farther. Do you do that?"

She made to turn but didn't quite. He didn't quite

answer either. It had never occurred to him before, but this dotty, middle-aged aunt must know things about his mother that no one else on earth did. She had already been in school when his mum was born. They'd played together, shared rooms, holidays, visits to relatives, upsets and illnesses, all sorts of little pains and pleasures.

"Didn't get much snow on the beach where we grew up," Liney went on. "Hastings Old Town, just above the fishermen's cottages. The sea was our doorstep. Dad had a little boat with an outboard motor, and he took us out all the time. Well, me some of the time, Lexie a lot. She was the apple of his eye from the moment she was born. I felt quite pushed out sometimes. He never really wanted me." She said this very matter-of-factly, glancing over her shoulder at him. "Born out of wedlock."

"So was I," Alaric said. "Mum and Dad didn't get married till almost a year after I was born."

"Ah, but things were different in the early sixties. Three or four years later it wasn't so end-of-the-world, and by the 1990s it was virtually compulsory. My dad was a bit of a throwback in any case. Not such a throw-back that he couldn't have his wicked way with an innocent eighteen-year-old, mind, and arrange for the result to be disposed of when he put her in the club."

"Disposed of?"

"Perhaps I shouldn't be talking to you about such things."

"It's okay." He managed not to sound too interested.

Liney turned back to the window; leaned so close to it that her nose very nearly rested on it.

"Mum told me much later. I mean *much* later. Probably thought I could handle it at twenty-eight. She overestimated me. To learn right out of the blue that your father wanted you terminated . . . hard to take at any age, I reckon. Almost got his way, too. Booked her into a clinic in Brighton, it was all set, but then, at the very last minute, for one of the few times in her life, she stood up to him. Refused to go through with it. I was that close— that close!—to not being here today, or yesterday, or any of the past forty-something exhilarating years."

He was only half listening. His mind was reeling.

All the stuff she knew about his mother. Stuff she never spoke about. Stuff no one ever asked to hear.

"What was she like?" he blurted.

Liney jumped out of her reverie. "Who?"

"Mum. When she was young."

"How young?"

"My age? Bit older?"

"You mean was she special in some way? Out of the ordinary?"

"No . . . " But he did.

Liney turned around and leaned against the table, facing him.

"My kid sister was clever as custard. Always. From the start. Not in the mathematical genius sense, but what an imagination, what aptitude. She was always designing things, and making things, amazing things. Gifted isn't the word. She could have done an awful lot, you know. Been anything she wanted. And you know what she wanted to be?"

"No, what?"

"Nothing but what she was. I swear she hadn't an

ambition in the world, that girl, which was a mite frustrating for a total incompetent like me who longed to see her name in lights. And she wasn't only more talented than anyone has a right to be, she had all the boys after her too. They used to troop up the path in droves, hoping for a smile or a wave or the touch of her hand. Your grandpa had to beat them off with a putter. Even those he allowed over the doormat sloped off with broken hearts in pretty short order."

"Why, what happened?"

"Lexie didn't see the point of boys. Men either, when she was older. Most, anyway. Very selective young woman. I have no *idea* what she saw in your father. She could have had her pick of anything in trousers, while I couldn't have gotten a blind date with Jabba the Hutt. I would have killed to have your mother's charms." She pushed herself away from the table. "I'll tell you something, though." Her eyes were suddenly very bright. "I don't half miss her."

"Do you?"

"Oh, yes. I miss her every day, every hour, every

minute of my sad little life." She went to the door, from where she gave him a small, tight smile. "Almost forgot. I was looking for you to ask if there's anything you don't eat. Seeing as I'm resident chef for a couple of days, may the gods preserve you, it's as well that I know what you won't touch with a barge pole before I put it in a pie."

His mind went blank. He couldn't recall a single thing he liked or disliked. "Can't think," he said truthfully.

"Good, so I can dish up anything I want. What do you say to cat's kidneys in cowpat gravy?"

"Yum."

Liney plucked his snowy socks from the door handle and slung them over her shoulder. "Poor lad thinks I'm joking," she said, and left him.

6.6

When Withern Rise was built in the first half of the 1880s, the kitchen was intended solely for the use of the cook, the housekeeper, and a general skivvy called Rosie, all of whom entered by a separate door from the garden. This door was also used by Bernard, the gardener and handyman, ever partial to a spot of slap and tickle with Cook. There'd been no servants at Withern for more than seventy years, the garden door to the kitchen had been filled in during the 1940s, and these days, at Naia's version of the house at least, the cook, housekeeper, skivvy, and gardener (and more often than not the handyman) took the single form of Alex Underwood. Alex's kitchen had recently been fitted with new cupboards built by a local cabinetmaker, and the old range had been replaced by a large gas stove. Alex cooked because she enjoyed it much of the time, and she was quite enjoying it this morning while wondering why Naia was continually drifting in and out and staring at her. How could she even dream that her daughter had been given an insight into an alternative family life that did not include her mother?

"Have I grown a second head overnight?" she asked. "Can't seem to take your eyes off me today."

"Flour on your nose," Naia replied.

"Oh, Naia, isn't there *anything* you can do?"

"Wipe it off yourself."

Naia drifted upstairs. About to enter her room, she noticed that the storage-room door was slightly ajar. When she was small she used to push back this door with a quickening pulse. To her, then, this small room was a place of shadow and mystery. The mysteries were contained in the accretion of boxes, old trunks, cases, and bags that virtually filled it. She used to, occasionally, open or dip into one of these and be fascinated by many of the things she found inside—coarse brown blankets, medals from wars she knew nothing about, gas masks that smelled of age and rubber, rusty camping equipment, and a lot of ancient family stuff her parents had no use for but lacked the heart to throw out. The attic contained similar jumble, but the storage room was more accessible than the attic, and just a few steps from her room, which, for a girl like Naia, born with an indefatigable curiosity, had made it worth peeking in to every now and then, sniffing around, lifting a cover, examining.

Entering the storage room today, she thought that

nothing much had changed since she last looked six months ago and was about to close the door when she saw the suitcase. She'd seen it before: Her mother had hauled it out of the attic a while back and gone through it looking for old documents, letters and suchlike, hoping to find more names and dates for the family tree she was compiling for the back of the photo album. Being at something of a loose end, Naia laid down the old brown suitcase and flipped the catches beside the handle. She raised the lid. A bygone fusion of camphor, sandalwood, and lavender wafted out, and the tiniest whiff of those small multicolored sweets that her late great-grandmother called *cachous* and kept in her handbag.

The contents of the suitcase were much as expected: small sepia and black-and-white photos, a stamp album, a wooden whistle with a pea in it (she tried it; it still worked), and papers of various kinds. There was also a very old magazine, *The County Journal*, from which, when she flipped it open, a slim cutting of discolored newspaper—an obituary—fluttered. She opened the magazine at the article the cutting had marked and found a folded drawing there. She studied the obituary, the article, and the drawing.

THE STONE GAZETTE
June 27, 1905

OBITUARY

The death has been announced of Aldous Lyman Underwood, former bishop of Eynesford and Stone. Mr. Underwood was still respectfully referred to as the Bishop by former parishioners at the time of his death, even though his last nine years were passed in retirement. He is survived by his wife, Elvira, and their son, Eldon. The Bishop is to be interred in the garden of his home, Withern Rise, beside the Great Ouse. Mrs. Underwood has announced her intention of planting an oak sapling over the body of her husband, in commemoration of his life and good works.

The article in *The County Journal* contained two photos, one of Aldous Underwood, haughty and unsmiling for the camera, but with the hint of a twinkle in his eye; the other of Withern Rise, ivy covered and rather grand looking, presumably taken the year the article was written.

THE COUNTY JOURNAL

August 1922

PHILANDERING BISHOP
BURIED IN "GROUNDS"

Characters from our county's past, number 14

Aldous Lyman Underwood, Bishop of Stone and Eynesford, had a reputation as a "ladies' man"—a well-deserved one, if the stories are to be believed. For Bishop Underwood is said to have bedded every half-comely woman of his diocese, unmarried or married, and sired several children who at baptism received names other than his.

According to press reports of the time, the Bishop (as he was known until his death in 1905) orchestrated his own fall from grace by making advances to one Joan Longridge while her husband, a wealthy grain merchant, was away on business. When Mr. Frank Longridge discovered that he had been cuckolded in his absence, and by a churchman for whom he had small regard at the best of times, he went to the Bishop's Palace with the intention of horsewhipping him round the grounds. Fortunately for the Bishop servants came to his rescue, but Mr. Longridge wasn't one to be so easily thwarted. He reported the transgressor to his archbishop, who, himself having little fondness for the flamboyant Underwood, was pleased to suspend him pending investigation. Investigation proved unnecessary, however, for by this time others in the community had come out against the Bishop, and he resigned his office rather than have his entire catalogue of misdemeanors exposed to public scrutiny.

Some years previously, in the early 1880s, the Bishop had acquired a substantial swathe of willowland on a tranquil bank of the Ouse by Eynesford village, cleared most of the ground, and built a fine house for himself and his wife and his only legitimately begotten son. He called the house Withern, which is believed to be Old English for "house in a willow wood," but two years after the building's completion the river rose dramatically and flooded the garden and the ground floor of the house, whereupon he renamed it Withern Rise. The Bishop appears to have been too attached to his home to consider abandoning it, and it was here that he spent his final years. It cannot have been an altogether easy retirement, for his erstwhile flock, freed of the obligation to show him the slightest respect, mockingly referred to his much-reduced diocese—his own property—as the Underwood See.

Upon his death at the age of sixty-nine, Underwood's wife, Elvira (having turned a surprisingly blind eye to his adulteries), had him interred in the grounds of his beloved house. She planted a young oak tree over him, which she called Aldous's Oak. The Bishop's son, Eldon, a widower, lives at Withern Rise to this day, with his own son (another was killed in the Great War) and two daughters. When asked about his father's reputation, Mr. Underwood said, "I'd rather not dredge all that up again, if you don't mind."

But he smiled fondly as he said it.

The pen-and-ink drawing that accompanied the obituary and the article was signed "Elvira." It was a map of sorts, shaded and embellished by someone with artistic pretensions but little ability, showing the spot in the south garden where she had laid her husband to rest and planted the oak sapling.

6.7

It was Liney's idea. "Let's walk along the river. I've never been here when everything's been under snow before." He immediately thought of half a dozen things he'd rather be doing, and people he'd rather be doing them with, but he found excuses elusive, and before he knew it he was putting his coat and boots on alongside her at the hall stand. He just hoped none of his mates would see him. Walkies with Aunty; he'd never live it down. In hope of avoiding this horror of horrors, he suggested that they go to Withy Meadows. It was so open there that if anyone he knew strayed that way he would spot them before they got too close and have a chance to make a break for it.

By the time they set out it was snowing harder than ever. Alaric kept his head well inside the hood of his parka, but Liney, though she wore a head scarf, revelled in the snow powdering her nose and cheeks. They left by the main gate at the end of the drive and followed the path to the longbow-shaped pedestrian bridge over the river five or six hundred yards along. Once they reached the bridge, Liney sprang upon it and stalked up its long easy slope like an ungainly three-year-old trying out new boots. At the halfway point she stopped and planted her elbows on the snow-thickened rail and looked back toward the house, the only dwelling to be seen before the river disappeared into the trees and bushes along the western bank.

"Isn't it beautiful?" Liney said of the view as Alaric caught up with her. "Isn't it *gorgeous*?"

Ill equipped to comment on the view's beauty or gorgeousness, he merely grunted as he plodded past her and down the slope of the bridge.

The vast landscaped area on the other side, known as Withy Meadows since its inception in the 1960s, was divided by numerous reedy channels and ponds dotted with small tousled islands thick with wildlife. There were also a number of walkways, so spaced out that there was little risk of bumping into anyone else, if that was your wish. Alaric had been a frequent visitor to the Meadows these past two years. Occasionally during his solitary walks, he forgot to scowl and slouch and feel sorry for himself; but then he would snap back to the reality he knew only too well and chastise himself for forgetting how shitty life was. Today he wanted to be alone for a different reason. He had a lot to think about, and he couldn't begin to—

A thump between the shoulder blades.

"Gotcha!"

He spun around. Liney squatted at the foot of the bridge, packing snow with her enormous mittens. The silly woman was chucking snowballs at him! Her arm rose. He backed away, hands stretched before him— "Whoa! No. No."—but Liney had him in her sights, and a second missile hurtled toward him. He ducked just in time, protesting that he didn't want to fight.

"Tough titty," Liney replied, gathering more snow.

Snowball number three lacked the accuracy of the first two, but it certainly connected. He buckled. A snowball in the balls.

"Oops!" Liney said. "Didn't mean that. You all right?"

"Oh, wonderful."

"So do your worst!"

"Listen . . . " he said feebly, straightening up.

"This is no time for idle chatter," she said, shaping another mittenful.

He glanced around. They were quite alone in the boundless Arctic waste. Snowball number four whizzed past his ear.

"Right," he said. "You asked for it."

He stooped, impacted snow into a hard ball, and stomped toward her while perfecting it. Liney looked up. "Hang on, not ready," she said.

"Nor was I," he replied, lobbing the snowball. It glanced off her arm, but Liney, an inveterate overreactor, shrieked as if he'd thrown a bucket of icy water over her. Then she said: "So!"

And that was it. All hell broke loose.

6.8

Naia had made up her mind. She would go and see Alaric. She had things to talk over with him. Things she couldn't talk to anyone else about. But she also wanted to let him know how much she sympathized with him; that she understood what it must be like for him without his mother. She couldn't just phone him to say she was on her way, though, or knock on a door down the street. No, there was only one way to reach him—if it worked both ways. She stood before her mother's Folly, wondering what you had to do. What had he done, the one time she'd witnessed his departure? His hands had been around the dome, but there had to be more to it than that, surely. To find out, she placed her hands on the glass, closed her eyes, and waited. She gave it a minute, then squinted around. The room hadn't changed. She closed the squinting eye again and said, "Take me there, take me there, take me there," over and over again.

Nothing continued to happen.

After more attempts and more failures, she began to get annoyed. Why wouldn't it work? *He'd* made it work, so why couldn't she? She wasn't doing this entirely for herself, after all. Part of her mission was to show sympathy for another. That was a good thing to do, wasn't it? A considerate and selfless act? Her hands were still spread around the dome when she said, with some passion: "I have to *see* him!"

The tingle in her hands startled her, but she left them where they were, imagining that Alaric had experienced this very sensation when visiting and leaving her. She was on the verge of feeling rather pleased that things were going according to plan after all when a pain like no other she'd ever known leaped up her arms and exploded in her chest. She fell backward and down, hit the floor, where, eyes closed in agony, she did not see the changes taking place, or even feel the first of the snowflakes on her skin. Only when the pain eased a little did she notice the drop in temperature and open her eyes.

She was sitting on snow-covered grass, in the garden.

She got up, breathing raggedly, gaping all about. Twice Alaric had visited her, and on neither occasion had he said anything about stopping off in the garden on the way. She might have guessed something of the sort from the snow on his slippers, but she hadn't. Amazingly, she hadn't. A thought occurred to her. If his house was identical to hers, his garden must be too. Hadn't he said that he'd known the view from her bedroom window all his life? Well, then. This looked like her garden, but suppose it wasn't? Suppose it was his, along with the house? But if all this belonged to Alaric's family rather than hers, there would have to be a *few* differences. They might be very minor ones, but she, with her mother's eye for detail, should be able to pick them out. She was right. Once suspected, the differences simply flew at her: the still-painted doors, the rubbish on the step (which her mother would *never* allow), the grounds themselves. Mum had recently acquired a part-time gardener, a Mr. Knight, who had knocked on the door offering his services early in January. Between them, Mr. Knight and her mother had tidied and prepared much of the garden for winter. No part of the garden in which Naia stood had been tidied. The thickening blanket of snow that covered almost everything could not conceal the fact that it hadn't been given any attention at all for several seasons.

But even if she'd failed to spot some of the differences, there was one she could not have missed. The ivy that scrambled across the walls of her house was kept in reasonable order all year round. Her mother usually let it go a bit in autumn—"Little treat for it," she would say—but cut it back in late November. The ivy on the house before her bulged around the drainpipes, fattened the window ledges, hung from the guttering in thick green-and-white drapes. She saw, too, looking up, that one of the chimneys was slightly twisted. They'd had a chimney like that until last summer, when her parents had called in a builder to take a look at it. The builder had pronounced it unsafe and rebuilt it without delay. He had also advised them to have the slates checked because a few were loose, and he'd been asked to see to them as well. Naia doubted that any builder had been contacted here, about the chimney or the roof.

All this she saw from the shelter of the Family Tree. Alaric's Family Tree, though it looked exactly like hers. The enormous span and spread of the boughs afforded little protection from the cold, which was already wheedling its way into her thin clothing. She wrapped her arms about herself and wondered how to get into the house. How had Alaric gotten into hers? He'd done it twice, so it couldn't be *that* hard. Angry with herself for not being able to guess what to do next, she decided against standing there hoping something would happen while she froze to death. If Alaric's Folly wasn't going to pull her into his house, she would take a more traditional route. His dad was in Newcastle, he'd told her, which meant that he was alone in the house. Another difference. Her parents would never leave her at home by herself for more than a few hours, even though she was sixteen. There'd been times when this had really annoyed her. Not today.

She bundled herself up and sprinted across the open lawn toward the door. On the step beside the untidy tower of boxes and shopping bags full of papers, she bent to push back the brass letter flap and peer into the hall. How uninviting it looked in there, how dull and gloomy. "Hello?" she shouted through the flap. "Alaric?" It was the first time she'd spoken his name, and it sounded strange to her, almost impertinent. But when no reply was returned, she tried again. "Alaric, it's me, Naia. Let me in, it's freezing out here!"

She listened. Nothing. No hint of life. No movement or sound. She straightened up; put her thumb on the bell. The manic arrangement of notes bounded through the house in vain.

She gave up. Nothing else for it. Put her back against the door and slithered down to squat on her heels. From this lowly position she noticed three pairs of footprints heading away from the door, and one approaching. The approaching pair and one of the departing pairs probably belonged to the milkman or the postman. She could only account for one of the other departers, whom she assumed to be Alaric. There was no telling when he'd be back, so shouldn't she find somewhere to shelter until then?

Where?

The most sheltered place she could think of was the porch on the river side of the house, but if she tucked herself in there, she wouldn't see or hear him return. There had to be somewhere on this side. The garage? At home, when the car was out, the garage doors were often left unlocked. Maybe here, too. She leaned out to look around the teetering tower of boxes and accidentally jogged them. The stack swayed. The top box toppled. It had very little in it, but she jumped when it hit her. She lashed out at it, inadvertently bumping the rest of the pile so that it collapsed about her. The step was now even more of a mess, but she didn't care. It wasn't her step. The only thing she was sorry about was that among all these boxes there wasn't one big enough to crawl into.

Shivering badly, and too despondent to go and check out the garage, she settled on the concrete ledge below the door, drawing her knees into her chest, enclosing them with her arms. The snow fell on the

boxes, the bulging bags, on her, and time began to
pass. She saw how it was going to be. When Alaric
eventually returned he would find this big white lump
surrounded by snowy box shapes on the step. Clearing
away the snow he would discover her, frozen solid,
blue skinned, eyes staring sightlessly. He would have
to report her death, but he wouldn't be able to say who
she was or that he knew her. No one would believe the
truth anyway, and she would be such a pathetic pinch-
faced object that the likeness to him would go completely unnoticed. She would be disposed of as an
unknown person, a stray asylum seeker or something,
probably in an unmarked grave or plastic urn. But
even that wasn't the worst of it. Back home, around
teatime, her mother would start to worry. She would
call the police. There would be a nationwide search for
her, but she wouldn't be found, and her parents would
spend the rest of their lives shuffling about in great
sorrow, certain their darling daughter had been
abducted, raped, strangled, and dumped in some
quarry, ditch, or swamp. And to cap it all . . . to cap it

all, her nose was running. She wiped it on her sleeve and turned to the tatty front door, beseeched it with all her heart to let her in, let her in, let her *in!*

If she'd only known, that was all she had to do. The garden quivered as though losing its hold on reality. Walls sprang up about her, replacing the front door and the step and the boxes. A ceiling obscured the gray sky, the snow stopped falling. She was sitting on the carpet of a River Room that was not her own, and before her, on a dusty sideboard, stood a Folly badly in need of a polish. She got to her feet. Very, very slowly.

She quickly noticed that this River Room was not only not much warmer than the garden, but as dismal as a room can be. She knew every stick of furniture in it, and the carpet, the curtains, the lamp, every ornament and photo and picture on the wall. Her own River Room had been like this until quite recently, though never as dowdy or dusty or unpleasant smelling. She perched on the edge of the faded blue chaise and eased her feet out of her snow-rimmed slippers, wriggling toes that felt as if they were about to drop off. Breathing on her hands, she gazed around her with a leaden heart.

"And he said it was the *same*."

She almost dreaded leaving that icy room to see what else this alternative Withern Rise had to offer. What little else.

6.9

Liney's approach to snowball warfare was hit and miss to say the least, but surprisingly effective. Alaric's style was more methodical and concentrated. Recovering from her most recent assault he would pursue her with as much speed as his self-conscious stride would allow. When accurately targeted Liney would squeal horribly and rush toward him, unleash her next volley, and gallop off like a demented giraffe, legs flying in all directions at once. Before long, the intensity of the conflict scuppered Alaric's inhibitions, and he was running this way and that, trying to head her off or avoid her, crouching behind trees and bushes as she did, yelling almost as loudly as her. It was well over two years since he'd last let himself go like this.

6.10

From Alaric's dreary River Room Naia stepped into the hall viewed minutes before from the other end, through the mail slot.

"Hello?"

Her voice, fragile with dismay, reached timidly into distant, cobwebby corners of the house; found nothing but an eerie, haunted silence. The floor felt gritty under her cold feet as she crossed it, shivering. The staircase that rose to her left was sorely in need of polish, and she'd never expected to see that stair carpet again. The lofty stair wall was the same tired green theirs had been before they got the decorators in. She knew all the pictures on it. Almost every one was slightly crooked, unlike at home. Her mother was fanatical about pictures being straight. Naia reached up to adjust the nearest one. Dust flew off the frame and stung her eyes.

Adjacent to the stairs, opposite the River Room, was one of the two doors to the Long Room. She went in, feeling very much the intruder. At home this was one of the favorite rooms, lightest in summertime, coziest in winter, with French windows opening onto the south garden. The room earned its name, stretching from the front to the back of the house, or from the back to the front, depending which way you looked at it. The room that met Naia's eyes was a sad mockery of the one she knew and loved. Rugs were rucked up, curtains hung badly because of lost or broken hooks, furniture had been nudged out of alignment by Underwood males stretching their legs and not bothering to put things back. At the end of every day Naia's mother would go around straightening things, thumping cushions back into shape, ironing out rumpled material with the flat of her hand. Here the cushions were squashed and badly creased, and *nothing* was straight.

Her sadness did not abate in the least as she walked through the room and stood before the old oak fireplace. At home, the mantel shelf above the fireplace was dotted with small mementos from various outings and holidays. This mantel's mementos had been supplanted by a tube of extra-strong mints, a large box of matches, a couple of packets of fuses, and a screwdriver. The Westminster clock was still at the center, but its hands were frozen at twenty past five. Of all times. The clock needed winding every seven days, so it could have stopped at any five twenty, A.M. or P.M., during the past two years. Its half-hourly chime might have been silent since the terrible event that had changed everything here.

The hearth was even more hideous, full of screwed-up bits of paper and spent matches, while the grate was a mass of cigarette butts. Naia had stood before the same fireplace less than an hour ago, enjoying its glow, feeling its warmth. During seasons in which extra warmth was not required, Mum put dried flowers here, meticulously arranged. Here, no flowers, no fire, just a sooty grate full of stubs. Her dad used to smoke, but he'd given up shortly after Mum came home from the hospital. His idea, no one else's. He'd persuaded himself that he owed it to her not to smoke around her while she wasn't well and had never taken it up again. There'd been no such incentive here.

She left the room and started upstairs. She no longer called out. The oppressive silence made her feel as if the house were watching her, storing a record of her every movement in its grim walls. With every upward step she felt sorrier and sorrier for Alaric, and angrier and angrier with his father—*her* father, in a way. She was certain that anything his dad did, hers would have done, or failed to do, in the same circumstances. And she had to ask herself how she might have responded if it had been her mother that had died. Would she have let everything go like this? Would she have just moped around and let her world fall apart? She liked to think she wouldn't, but how could she be sure? Would anyone ever be the same if their life was thrown so cruelly off track? Track. Railway line. That was what had started all this. A crack in the line. Such a small thing, but what a devastating result! A train hurled skyward, carriages twisted and crushed, small injuries to many, fatal ones to others, Alaric's mother among them. A crack in the family line. A crack that widened and widened, deepened and deepened, day after day, until . . . this.

Four bedrooms opened out from the landing, plus the storage room, the bathroom, and, up a small extra flight of stairs, the long space under the slope of one of the roofs that served as the attic. Naia headed for the corner bedroom, the room she occupied at home. Although she had no doubt that she was alone in the house, she couldn't help but tap on the door. When, as expected, this elicited no response, she pushed the door back—and right away wished she hadn't. In her version of this room she'd had trouble finding space for all her stuff in recent years. She could have moved to a larger room, but the one she'd always had was special to her, with its views of the river from one window, the south garden from the other. She kept it clean and reasonably tidy, tried to make it interesting in various ways, liked to feel when she entered that it not only welcomed her but couldn't possibly belong to anyone else. Clearly, Alaric didn't have similar feelings. His room was very messy, very shabby, so "can't-be-bothered." Drawers had been left open, clothes were slung any old where, the bed was unmade. There were chocolate wrappers on the floor.

She went back along the landing to the bathroom and felt physically sick when she looked in. Horrible smell, mean little bits of soap, dirty towels bunched on the wooden rack, smeared mirror, torn plastic shower curtain, tiny hairs rimming the bath, plug dangling from a piece of brown string. She left quickly.

In the guest bedroom she encountered a mystery. At home they had no visitors at present, but someone was definitely ensconced in this room. It smelled artificially pleasanter than the other rooms, and a hasty attempt had been made to tidy it, though the occupant seemed to have no sense of order, and even less taste. The few articles of rather outlandish attire that hung from the rod at one end looked as if they belonged to either a madwoman or a drag artist. A large patchwork bag leaned against a turquoise suitcase. The suitcase was covered with butterfly transfers, and the shapeless bag, made up of clashing patches, had one handle larger than the other.

Naia saved the master bedroom for last. This should have been the most elegant room in the house, but there was nothing elegant here; not anymore. It smelled of stale sweat, cigarette smoke, dirt. The curtains were carelessly drawn. The duvet and pillows were grubby. On the floor, randomly scattered, were several pairs of scuffed shoes. Beside the bed, there were two overflowing ashtrays, and an empty whiskey bottle.

Something metallic stuck out from under the bed. She stooped to see what it was. A dusty rowing machine. Her dad had one just like it. Same type, color, probably the same serial number. He'd bought it three or four years ago and used it as little as possible. Every so often Mum told him he was putting it on around the middle, and he hauled the machine out and worked at it for about ten minutes before shoving it out of sight again. It was a long time since this one had been given a ten-minute workout.

Naia stared forlornly about her. At home this was a

beautifully coordinated, ultra-cozy bedroom; the only really old-fashioned room in the house, deliberately so, full of parlor palms and jardinières, lacy shawls draped along bamboo screens, old postcards in little silver frames. Under one of the windows there was a padded seat on which her mother liked to curl up and read sometimes. In summer and autumn the window was shaded by the shifting fronds of the willow beyond. It felt like company, Mum said. Her father had never seemed to mind that their room wasn't very masculine. Gazing at this shoddy clone of that infinitely calm, attractive room, Naia understood why for the first time: he didn't *care* what it was like—or what became of it.

A massive burr walnut wardrobe took up most of one wall. Her eye was caught by the left-hand door, which wasn't quite closed. The wardrobe being a precise duplicate of the one in her parents' room, she knew that it contained three compartments.

She pulled back the partially open door and revealed a disarray of crumpled trousers and jackets and half a dozen shirts that would have benefited from an intro-duction to an iron. Two of the shirts were frayed at the cuffs, and one had a tidemark around the inside collar. The narrow middle part of the wardrobe, over which the two large doors met, was equipped with a number of shelves and shallow drawers. This was where her mother put their clean underwear and hankies, inter-spersed with fragrant little bags of herbs or lavender. The central section of the present wardrobe contained no fresh linen, no fragrances, just bundles of dirty clothes.

Naia gripped the handle of the right-hand door, Alaric's mother's side, and opened it slowly, dreading what she would find within. She found very little: a tangle of hangers on the rod, and on the floor, among several balls of fluff, a pair of small brass binoculars, quite old. What had they done with her things? Burned them? Given them to a charity shop? It was as if they'd tried to wipe out all memory of her.

She closed the door with haste and went to the stool before the marble-topped washstand that Alaric's mother—like hers, still—had used as a dressing table. She put her elbows on the white-veined gray marble and her chin in her palms, and stared helplessly into the large oval mirror on the wall. The dismal face in the slightly speckled glass might have been Alaric's. No wonder he's bitter, she thought. How he must resent me.

She lowered her eyes, unable to look at that wounded, grieving, accusing face any longer. She'd always loved the things Mum kept on the marble top: little cut-glass scent bottles, decorative hat pins in a velvet cushion, mother-of-pearl combs, a tortoiseshell hand mirror, small boxes and trays for rings and bracelets and trinkets. Nothing very valuable, but all very pleasing to the eye. There were none of these things here. They had been supplanted by a clutter of felt-tipped pens, torn tickets, mouth sprays, coins, books of matches, a couple of dog-eared John Grishams. It was all so ugly. The whole place was ugly. The lives of the people who lived here were ugly.

"This isn't my house!"

Alaric's words on realizing that he'd stumbled into a

more cherished Withern Rise. What a shock it must have been for him. She couldn't blame him for being so desperate to get away. But to this! There must be something I can do, Naia thought. There has to be *something*.

Then it came to her. There was something.

She got up at once, and started.

6.11

Liney had been simmering something alarmingly pungent in the largest saucepan she could find. "Gives me more burn room," she said to Alaric, who was still as suspicious of her sense of humor as he was unconvinced of her culinary expertise. When she estimated that it was ready, she put a bowl in front of him and one in front of herself at the other end of the kitchen table.

He sniffed the bowl's contents. "What is it?"

"I call it soup. Try it."

"After you," he said.

"Be bold, nephew. You might be pleasantly surprised."

He sampled it. When he looked up, his eyes were

very wide.

"I've never tasted anything like it."

She smiled broadly. "New recipe."

"Where from?" She tapped the side of her head. "Oh, that explains it."

He took another dutiful sip in case some of his taste buds had been faulty. No, they'd all been on full power. He put his spoon down.

"Sorry, I can't."

Liney tasted hers. Her face, too, adopted a pained expression. "There's a lot of goodness in it," she said by way of compensation.

"It's the flavor I have a problem with."

He pushed his bowl away and went to the freezer for a pizza. He removed the wrapper and popped the pizza in the microwave. Some minutes later, when he was well into it, Liney, a game three-quarters of the way through her soup, suddenly said: "You know, this is disgusting."

"There's another pizza if you want it," he said.

"I mean the kitchen. The entire house. How could

he have let it go like this?" Alaric toyed with a coin of pepperoni. Guilt by association. "Perhaps I'll run the vacuum over it and dust a few things," Liney said. "Someone ought to."

She narrowed her gobstopper eyes at him, clearly hoping for an offer. "Sorry," he said. "Homework." He bolted the rest of his pizza.

Going upstairs, Alaric noticed the smell of polish. The banister gleamed and felt unusually smooth under his hand. Entering the bathroom, he lifted the toilet seat and saw a rare swirl of disinfectant around the bowl. Then he noticed that the bath and basin were clean, and that the little slivers of soap had been replaced by a new bar from the cupboard. The towels had been straightened, too, and the bath mat had been draped neatly over the side of the bath, and the manky old shower curtain had been hooked up in the three places it had been unhooked for months. All this he put down to his aunt, though he couldn't think when she'd found the time. They'd been playing silly buggers at Withy Meadows until early afternoon, and it hadn't been like this before they went out. As if to claim responsibility for the transformation, Liney, half-heartedly accompanied by Tom Jones, started belting out "Sexbomb" in the kitchen. Alaric couldn't help a small laugh as he strolled along the landing to his room.

He had no more intention of catching up on his homework than pole-vaulting to the moon, but he took care to set the scene in case he was disturbed. An hour later he was lying on his bed, swaddled in his duvet and surrounded by schoolbooks while music pumped into his ears through a headset. The music soundtracked his thoughts; thoughts that, wherever they wandered, returned constantly to the other Withern Rise—and the voice from the bottom of the stairs. He didn't hear the door open because of the music, and he didn't see it open because his eyes were closed. The first he knew that he was no longer alone was the hand on his shoulder. His eyelids flew back. Liney was leaning over him.

"Sorry to startle you," she said as he tore the headset from his ears. "I did knock. Couldn't seem to make myself heard." She flicked one of the untouched schoolbooks. "The studies proceeding apace, I see."

"I was taking a break." He discarded the duvet and sat up, swinging his feet off the bed. "What did you want?"

"Only to let you know how impressed I am," she said.

"Impressed?"

"When I looked in your father's room yesterday I thought it had been hit by terrorists. Imagine the shock when I went in just now to try and sort it out. The bathroom too. When did you *do* all that?"

"I haven't the faintest what you're talking about."

Liney grinned conspiratorially. "Don't worry, I won't tell on you. Wouldn't want the old man making it a regular assignment, would we?" She went to the door. "I'm vacuuming the landing. I'll want to do in here in a min. Okay with you?"

He shrugged, and she closed the door. The noisy vacuum cleaner started up outside. He sat listening to it fade into the distance, then buzz around for a while at the other end of the landing before starting back. When it thudded against his door demanding to be let in, he got up and admitted it, jumping back as the cantankerous old beast snapped at his ankles. He slipped out and headed along the landing. He couldn't imagine what Liney thought he'd done to his dad's room, which was even more of a dump than his most of the time. He pushed the door back. The shoes previously scattered wherever they'd been kicked off now stood in a neat polished row under the window. The ashtrays had been emptied and cleaned. The dressing table was clear of all the rubbish. The curtains had been straightened. The room had even been sprayed with something that resembled the smell of overripe apples. Alaric could only stare. She thought *he'd* done all this? The woman was even more off her head than he thought. She must have done it herself, in her . . .

Oh.

He got it.

He was filled first with rage that Naia had taken it upon herself to do this, then humiliation that she'd seen the state of the place, which she would naturally have compared to her own perfect home. She must have felt so sorry for him, and so chuffed with herself for her "good deed." Alaric bunched his fists. Who the hell did she think she was? Well, she wouldn't get away with it. He'd put her in her place. Just you wait, he thought. Just you wait.

6.12

Naia would have stayed longer and done more, but she hadn't wanted her mother to start wondering where she'd got to. Also, the visitor with the dubious taste might have returned at any time. She hadn't fancied trying to explain herself to that one. The way back, she was pleased to discover, was easier than the outward journey, and pain free. All she had to do was put one hand or both hands on Alaric's Folly and think of home, whereupon the room faded and she was in the garden; her garden this time. The last leg was even less difficult. Want to be inside the house bad enough and there you were, in whichever room the Folly was at that time. Once back she laughed, thinking, My first visit to an alternate reality, and I tidy it up. But then she remembered Alaric's depressing house and his sad life, and the laughter died.

She spent much of the afternoon and early evening drifting from room to room, picking things up, sighing, putting them down again. If it looked to her mother as if she was taking some sort of mental inventory of the house contents, she wasn't far wrong. Naia was comparing her lot with Alaric's, thinking that if chance had gone the other way, in his favor instead of hers, their positions would have been reversed, and it would have been she who'd ended up living in a cheerless cold house with just one parent and an unpromising future.

6.13

When the hall phone rang that evening, it was Naia, passing, who picked it up.

"Hi, Nai, it's me."

"Hello," she said coolly.

"How's the weather there?"

"Wintry."

"Here, too. Snow's coming down harder than ever."

"I suppose you're with Kate," Naia said.

"Kate? Not right now, but we had dinner. That's why I'm ringing so late. Sends her love."

"I'm sure!"

"Sorry?"

"So you should be. *Mum*!" she yelled, hoping to deafen him. "Your husband's on the phone!"

She banged the receiver down on the hall table and flounced into the Long Room, where she threw herself on the couch and started flipping through the TV channels. A few minutes later her mother came in and flopped onto the big beanbag she'd placed beside the coffee table, where she was bringing the family album up to date. She'd started the album when carrying Naia, and several of the early pictures showed her in a maternity dress with a bump. She was very selective in her choice of pictures for the album. They were in strict sequence throughout, dated, and often humorously captioned. She liked each page to look different, which meant varying the shape and size of the prints as well as the layout. She kept scissors and a small paper cutter handy for this.

"Dad said you were a bit off," she said, sifting through the last of the prints on the table. "Wonders what he's done."

"Does he."

Naia paused briefly at a music quiz show, a documentary about the pyramids, and Johnny Depp as an opium-fueled Victorian detective hunting Jack the Ripper.

"Can't you settle on one?" Alex said.

"Nothing on."

"So turn it off."

She didn't turn it off, mainly because she'd been told to, but dithered at a stagy-looking play full of people in tunics. Alex looked up. *Oedipus Rex.* As a student she'd appeared in a production of that. The screen went blank. Naia tossed the remote aside and plucked an orange from the fruit bowl. She mooched over to the fire and remained there, casting peel to the flames. Silence for some time, then:

"Naia, have you seen the Folly?"

Naia's throat contracted on a piece of orange. She coughed to clear it.

"The Folly? Why?"

"Why? Because it's not where it belongs, that's why."

"I took it up to my room." It was all she wanted to say, but more seemed to be expected. "I'll put it back if it's such a big deal."

"It's not a big deal," Alex answered calmly. "I just like to know where things are. Which of these do you think I should put in?"

The Westminster clock started to chime as Naia pushed herself away from the mantelpiece. She leaned over the coffee table. The two pictures under consideration were among the most recent, taken just before Christmas, of her mother and father dolled up for a costume party. Mum was a female Santa Claus, beard and all; Dad was Frankenstein's monster, in big boots, bolt through his neck, and green fishnet tights (a personal innovation). The main difference between the two photographs was that in one her father stood hand on hip, pouting outrageously.

"That one," Naia said, indicating the other. "Looks less of a prat."

"Just as I thought," her mother said. "Sense of humor needs a service."

"Why ask if you're going to do what you want anyway?"

Alex looked at her. "Why don't you sit down here with me and tell me what's making you so edgy today?"

"I'm not edgy," Naia snapped.

"Oh. Really. I must be imagining it then."

She had no way of knowing that Naia longed to talk to her about the things on her mind but couldn't, simply couldn't, because of who she was. How could she tell her mother about another Alex Underwood who hadn't survived the train crash, about a Withern Rise falling apart through neglect, about Kate moving in with an alternate version of her father, who still smoked?

"You need something to keep your mind occupied,"

Alex said.

"My mind is occupied."

"With . . . ?"

She shrugged. "Stuff."

"Oh. Stuff."

Naia spat a couple of pits into her palm and threw them at the fire. The flames flared gratefully.

"Think I'll go to bed."

"At ten o'clock? You?"

"Nothing to stay up for." She drifted toward the far door.

"Oh, Naia."

Naia turned.

"The Folly?"

"I'll bring it down."

"No need. Keep it up there if you want. Just so I know."

Alex listened to her daughter plodding upstairs in leaden slippers. It was impossible to reach her when she was like this, but she was sixteen. Bottling things up and thinking your parents wouldn't understand went with the territory. She resumed her task. Minutes passed, marked by the regular ticking of the clock. But then, a shriek from upstairs, followed by a heavy thud. Alex jumped up, flew along the room to the far door, out into the hall.

"Naia?" She was already on the stairs when Naia appeared in the landing in her underwear. "Nai, what is it?"

"Tripped taking my jeans off. Fell over."

"Sounded as if you were being attacked."

"Only by my jeans."

"Well, don't frighten me like that!"

"Sorry."

Alex returned to the Long Room and the photo album.

Naia went back into her bedroom. "*Idiot!*" she said, closing the door behind her.

6.14

It was perfectly true that she'd fallen over while getting undressed. She had unzipped her jeans and extracted her left leg, and was stooping to untangle her right foot when the room went cold. Sensing some sort of presence behind her, she half turned and found a hooded figure in snow-covered boots standing there. This was when she shrieked and fell, caught in her jeans.

Returning from soothing her mother's fears, she followed "Idiot!" with "Don't look!" and snatched her dressing gown from the hook on the door. "What are you doing here at this time of night?"

Alaric turned away, opening his coat and nudging his hood back. It was boiling in here after his room and the garden. "Thought I'd stand more chance of finding you here now."

"Well, congratulations, you were right."

"Can I turn around yet?"

She tied a fierce bow in the belt of her dressing gown. "If you must."

He did so, determined to maintain the anger he'd been nursing for hours. "You came to my place today. Why?"

"I wanted to see if my Folly worked too."

"Clean up after us, you mean. What a bloody nerve!"

"Keep your voice down, Mum's just downstairs."

"What a bloody nerve," he repeated more quietly. "How would you like it if some snoop went around going through your stuff while you were out?"

"I'm not a snoop, and I didn't go through your stuff."

"Bet you had a good look."

"Don't flatter yourself. I'm not in the least interested in your stuff."

He scowled the last of his fury at her. His indignation sounded rather feeble now, even to him.

"Well don't ever clean up after us again, right?"

"If you feel like that about it I'll go and muck it all up again."

"Too late for that. My aunt's seen it. Thinks I did it."

"Your aunt?"

"I bet yours is still at home in Sheringham," he sneered. "Left in peace, *you*."

"I don't have an aunt in Sheringham."

The sneer vanished. "Eh?"

"I don't have an aunt anywhere."

"But everything's the same. Mum, Dad, the house. You must have an aunt." He leaned forward earnestly, as though earnestness would jog her memory. "Liney? Selina? Mum's older sister?"

"My mother hasn't got an older sister," Naia said. "And yours *has*?"

"Had. Only person I ever heard call my mother Lexie, apart from Mum herself. Liney and Lexie. Names they gave themselves as kids, she told me."

Naia couldn't get over it. "Why did your mother have a sister and mine didn't? I don't get it."

But Alaric got it. Got it only too well. "Mystery," he said, giving nothing away.

"And she's staying with you, this aunt? Is that her stuff I saw in the guest room?"

"Yes."

"I thought it was a mad person's."

"You weren't wrong."

"Is she married? Any kids?"

"No."

"How old is she?"

"Forty-three, forty-four, hundred and five, what does it matter?"

"What's she like? Tell me about her, I want to know everything."

"I don't want to talk about her."

"Oh, please. I want to hear."

"No."

At last he had something she hadn't. Someone. Liney might not be the dream relative, but she was his—his alone, as it turned out—and he was keeping her to himself. Realizing that he wasn't going to budge on this, Naia decided to leave it for now. Noticing lumps of slowly dissolving snow on the carpet, she felt around under the bed for the sheet of Christmas wrapping paper from last time. She also produced a rolled-up shopping bag containing his slippers.

"Didn't you miss these?"

"I was in a hurry."

"Well take them with you this time. A man's slippers under my bed could have caused me some headaches if Mum found them."

She spread the paper out on the floor. "Stand on this."

He didn't stand on it. He sat down on the bed and lifted his feet for her to slip the paper under them.

"Was that all you wanted when you came to mine?" he said. "To test your Folly?"

She dropped into the chair with the rip in the arm. "And to see you."

"Why? What for?"

"We have things to talk about."

"Yeah, suppose we do."

"Not least the Follies themselves, now that we know they both work."

"The Follies. Sounds like a cancan show."

She ignored this. "My mother made ours three or four years ago, so I suppose your mum made yours then too." He signaled confirmation. "I don't know about you," she went on, "but I must have touched ours dozens of times since then and nothing happened. So why now?"

"Just one of those things?" he ventured.

"Just one of those things! I've been doing some thinking about this, and I've come to the conclusion that the two Follies were activated by a combination of factors all coming together at the same time."

"Factors?"

She reached for a reporter's notebook on her bedside table.

"Mum told me that she thought the original shade belonged to the wife of the Underwood who built Withern Rise. That's factor one." She flipped open the notebook and consulted the list she'd compiled. "Factor two, the Underwood who built Withern is buried in the garden."

"What?"

"You didn't know that?"

"No."

"Nor did I till today. I was looking through an old suitcase in the storage room, and I came across an obituary and a magazine article about this randy churchman. Bishop Aldous something Underwood."

"*Bishop* Underwood?"

"Yes, our very own bish, and a naughty one at that. History of hanky-panky with the local wenches."

"And he's buried in your garden?"

"Mine and yours, I reckon. A version of him in each."

"Whereabouts?"

"The old boy's wife did a drawing. Didn't want a gravestone in the garden, I s'pose, so she planted a tree over him. Under-wood? Under-tree? Could be her idea of a joke, but I doubt it. I mean, she was in *mourning*, for God's sake."

"Is the tree still there?"

She got up and went to the window overlooking the south garden. He followed her, trailing small blocks of snow, looked over her shoulder.

"The Family Tree?"

"Has to be, going by the drawing. The Widow Underwood called it Aldous's Oak. Maybe someone who came after her wanted to forget who was down there and changed the name."

"I used to climb that tree all the time," Alaric said.

"Me too. Might not have if I'd known it was a grave marker."

She returned to the chair. "But if you think about it, it's right that he's there. I mean, if not for him Withern wouldn't exist, and neither would we. Not here anyway. That's factor three, by the way."

"What is?"

"That the Family Tree was planted over Bishop Aldous. And factor four is the *year* it was planted, which was also the year he died, of course."

Alaric went back to the bed and placed his feet on the Christmas wrapping paper. "Remind me."

Naia managed not to glare at the fresh trail of snow leading to and from the window. "1905. A century ago this very year. See how they come together?" She looked at her notebook. "Factor five—"

"How many of these are there?" he asked.

"Few more. Factor five, Alex Underwood made a model of Withern Rise, to put inside Widow

Underwood's shade. A model carved out of wood from the Family Tree. Factor six, the first time your Folly sent you here was the second anniversary of the railway accident in which . . . "

She didn't need to finish.

"I have another factor for you," Alaric said. "The night of the accident it started to snow—and it started snowing again yesterday."

"You think the snow's important?"

"Why shouldn't it be? Because I thought of it?"

"No, I mean does it *have* to be snowing? It might be a vital factor. It's been snowing each time you've come here, and it was snowing when I went to yours earlier. Maybe it has to be snowing for the Follies to work. Which means that if it stops you could be stuck here."

Alaric glanced at the window. "Have you heard the weather?"

"Not the local, but it's quite heavy in Bristol."

"Well, first sign of it easing off, I'm gone."

"You'd better be. A sudden male lodger in my room

might not go down too well with my parents."

"Question," he said.

"What?"

"If the Follies started working because all these factors came together on just the right day, yesterday, why are they still working today?"

Naia hiccupped a shoulder. "Maybe a link was forged between the Follies, and now that they're activated all we have to do is sort of . . . log on."

"You have an answer for everything, don't you?"

"Do my best. There's one more factor." She scribbled in the notebook. "Call it factor eight now we've added snow. You've used the Folly three times to get here, yes?"

"Yes, so?"

"On those three occasions, were you upset in any way? I mean angry, sad, particularly emotional?"

His expression darkened. Intrusion. She knew it, but went on regardless.

"When I tried to reach you, my Folly wouldn't work at first. But then I got annoyed, close to desperate, and suddenly I was in the garden. Your garden. You might have told me about that, by the way. I'd have put some warm things on. And the pain! Could have warned me about that, too."

"I didn't know you'd be dropping in."

"Well? Were you?"

"Was I what?"

"In a bit of a state those three times."

"No."

"You're sure?"

"*Yes.*"

She left it. Like the aunt, it would keep until he was in a more mellow mood. But there were other things that wouldn't keep.

"Want to know what else I've been thinking?" He said nothing, just sat there, waiting for the next flash of brilliance. "The night of the train crash. The derailment. Mum had a fifty-fifty chance, right?"

"Do we have to keep going back to that?" he said wearily.

"Sorry, but it's important. A fifty-fifty chance, live or die, and what did she do? She lived *and* died. There she is, on the train from King's Cross, and it hits that cracked rail, and suddenly her life's in the balance. It's so touch and go that reality can't handle it, so a second reality has to be created in order for both things—her life and her death—to happen at once."

"Created? Are we in Godland here?"

"No. Alternate realities are self-creating."

"You know this for a fact, do you?"

"Course not, I'm speculating."

"Which means it could be total bollocks."

"Could be. But there has to be some scientific explanation. You know the way a living cell divides in two? It splits, replicates itself, forms its own twin. Well imagine reality as one great big ginormous cell that in certain circumstances—life-threatening situations, say—becomes two, identical except that the event that caused the division turns out differently in each."

"Just like that?" he said.

"Just like that."

"Always a life-death situation?"

"Not necessarily. Might be a decision, a 'do I, don't I?'

moment. Take one course of action and this happens, take the other, and . . . " She put an invisible pistol to her temple. "Mum showed me a story in the paper a while back, about this man, dentist I think, not that it matters, who was driving home from work when he reached in his coat pocket for a stick of chewing gum. As he did so, a cat ran into the road. The man swerved, one hand still in his pocket, and he lost control of the car, drove onto the pavement, where a young couple with a toddler in a stroller were coming out of a real-estate agent's. He plowed into them, killed all three outright. Imagine. If he hadn't gone for the gum when he did, or if the cat hadn't run out, that family would have gotten safely home and the dentist wouldn't now be doing time for manslaughter."

"And in an alternate reality, they all live happily ever after," Alaric said.

"Happiness has nothing to do with it. This isn't some instant heaven thing, with everyone smiling to music through all eternity."

"These realities of yours . . . how close are they to

one another?"

"Close?"

"Physically."

"They occupy the same space. When we step from one into the other, we enter a different version of the very space we just left."

"They occupy the same space, but are invisible to one another?"

"They don't *exist* to one another. They're real only to themselves and the life forms in them. Some animals might sense another reality from time to time, though. Ever see a dog snarl at something that isn't there?"

"That's because dogs have Weetabix for brains."

"But pretty acute senses. Maybe the occasional human gets a glimpse, too. Think of all the people who've claimed to see spectral figures on staircases or standing at the foot of their bed. The young children heard crying in houses where there are no kids. How do we know these aren't peeks into neighboring or overlapping realities?"

"How can we see into them if they're completely

separate?"

"I don't know. Maybe there's a flaw here and there." She lifted her hand to show the rip in the arm of the chair. "Like a tear in a piece of fabric. Gives us the odd little glimpse, then . . . self-seals."

At this the incredulity he'd been fighting to keep inside for fear of seeming as dim and unimaginative as she made him feel, finally surfaced. "Where do you *get* all this stuff?"

She smiled. "Came to me in a dream."

Naturally, he thought she was joking. So did she.

"Look, we could speculate all night," Naia said then, "but Mum might come up at any time. Suppose we concentrate on us. Us and family. Like the aunt?" she added hopefully.

"Forget the aunt," he said curtly.

"You and me then. Like where we were born and all. I was born at Finchinglea Hospital, October fifth, 1988. You?"

"Fifth of October, 1988, Finchinglea Hospital."

"Time?"

He looked at his watch. "Almost half ten."

"Of birth," she said patiently.

"Mmm . . . 'bout five fifteen in the afternoon, I think."

She raised her eyebrows. "Five fifteen? Not five twenty?"

"Oh, yeah, that's it. How do you remember that?"

"Mum kept a baby book."

"So did mine, but I don't know it by heart."

"She shows it to visitors all the time in front of me."

His mother used to do that too, he recalled; a recollection he kept to himself.

"You know what this means, don't you?" Naia said.

"I'm sure you'll tell me."

"We're the same person."

"Uh?"

"Think about it. What else could we be?"

"How can we be the same? We're . . . "

"Different sexes, yes, but we're both the only child of Alex Underwood—Alex Bell, as she was then— born the same minute in the same place. We're variants of a single individual." He was still trying to take this in when she slapped her forehead. "Oh, I'm so *thick*! I've been thinking that all this started with the train crash. But that's not right. Can't be. It has to have started before that. Fourteen years before."

"Why, what happened then?"

"We happened. You and me."

"You think *we* started this double reality thing?"

"Makes sense to me," she said excitedly. There's one Alex Bell, right? She's pregnant, and like any mother-to-be who isn't into genetic engineering she might have either a girl or a boy. Because it's such a tight fifty-fifty thing a second reality has to kick in so she can have both simultaneously. Of course, neither Alex knows that there's now two of her, one with a girl, the other with a boy."

"A second reality would have started before birth," Alaric said.

"Yes, just before, goes without saying."

"No, long before. The baby's been growing inside her for months. It would have become male or female at conception."

Naia gaped. "Why didn't I think of that—"

"Quiet!"

She stopped, wide eyed.

"Someone on the stairs."

She listened. Stairs creaked. Naia jumped out of the chair like a marionette whose strings have been yanked. "Quick, under the bed!"

"I'm not getting under there," he said. "Stall her."

He went to the bookcase and put his hands around the Folly.

"Slippers!" She thrust them under his arm, then raced to the door and out to the landing to intercept her mother. She succeeded easily, because Alex was going to the bathroom, not coming to see her.

When she returned, all that was left to show that Alaric had been there was the trail of melting snow between the bed and the bookcase.

6.15

Late as it was, on his return Alaric went to the

storage room, curious to read the obituary and the article Naia had mentioned. He found no suitcase, but the room's weak forty-watt light did not penetrate far. Maybe it was under all the junk at the back or hiding in the shadows. Tomorrow, if he remembered.

In bed he went over the things they'd talked about. It rankled that Naia seemed so much cleverer than him, but he had to admit that some of her ideas were interesting. Her two-realities-out-of-one theory stretched the imagination, but if he accepted the proposition that a single reality could morph into two at some dramatic instant or point of decision, there was some satisfaction in it for him: that she was wrong about when it happened—and the cause. She had worked out that there were already two realities the night of the derailment. What she had not worked out—because she didn't have the informa-tion he had—was that there were two realities even before they were born. Twenty-seven years earlier a young woman had stood up to, or failed to stand up to, her future husband about an abortion he'd arranged. Because of her impulsive act of rebellion, the one reality, struggling to cope with an unanticipated turn of events, had become two. One to accommodate Liney Bell's birth; the other to absorb her nonexistence.

Part ②

The Parallel
Grave

Day Five

5.1

Going down a little earlier than usual next morning, Alaric was surprised to find his aunt warming her hands on the old kitchen range, which she'd lit an hour before. She was still dressed for subzero temperatures, however, in a padded blue anorak over her yellow dungarees, with a multicolored scarf encircling her neck twice and a pair of thick knitted socks bulging out of tartan flip-flops. It was so long since there'd been any real warmth in the house that Alaric registered pleasure before remembering that pleasure wasn't something he did these days and hunched his shoulders over his customary bowl of honey-nut cornflakes. Liney, having already consumed her daily portion of "grapefruit segments in pure apple juice," seated herself at the other end of the table to munch the wedge of whole-wheat toast she'd just burned to a lip-smacking crisp.

"When are they coming to look at the heating?" Alaric asked.

"Good question," she replied.

"I thought you'd arranged it."

"So did I. The man said he'd be here at eight-thirty, which I took to mean the first one of the day. I'd blame the snow, but he only lives in the village. I'll give him another half hour, then send you around to give him a piece of my mind."

"I'm not doing that!"

She grinned at him. Her teeth were black from the burned toast.

A minute or two later the phone rang in the hall. Liney was off her seat and out there before Alaric could blink. When she came back she said, "Your father. He's going to be delayed. Couple of extra days, he thinks."

"Why, what's happened?"

"It's been snowing there nonstop since yesterday, he says, and some of the roads are impassable."

"Probably an excuse," Alaric said uncharitably.

"Excuse for what?"

"What do you think?"

Liney sat down again. "We're managing, aren't we?" she said. "We can get by without your dad a bit longer."

"Don't you have to get back to the shop?"

"I shut the shop from the end of January to mid-March. Very little call for crafty stuff in Sheringham this time of year."

The prospect of two extra days in his aunt's company alarmed Alaric less than it would have done twenty-four hours earlier. She was, after all, someone who'd come "that close" to not existing, which made her more worth putting up with, somehow. Also, with his father away for two more days, he would be spared Kate's arrival that bit longer. Better loopy Liney than unwanted mother substitute Kate Faraday.

"But I can't just sit around in this ice house doing nothing," Liney said. "I'll go barmy if I don't keep myself occupied."

"Too late for that," he muttered.

"I heard that. What do you say to a spot of home decorating?" His eyes narrowed to suspicious slits. "Tart the dump up a bit in the little time we have. In tandem. The pair of us. Batbird and Dobbin."

"I'm no good at stuff like that."

"Well, neither am I, but I don't let it hold me back. Your mum used to keep all the painty things in that storage area over the garage, I remember. Know if they're still there?"

He shrugged dismally. "Never go up there." Decorating the house with Liney. Nightmares didn't get much more real than that. "I have to go out anyway," he said.

"You do?"

"Yes. Promised yesterday."

"Oh." She sounded disappointed.

He gulped the rest of his cereal and fled. Along the hall he popped into the River Room for the Folly and carried it carefully upstairs. In his bedroom he put it on top of the bookcase, as Naia had done. When he was dressed, he went down again, needing to make sure Liney was occupied. He was just in time to see her go out the front door. He went to the step and peered around the bags and boxes she'd restacked at some point; saw her lugging one of the garage doors back— no easy task with all the snow that had piled up against it in the past two days. She disappeared inside. Good, now he could claim to have left while she was going through the paint in the garage.

No, wait. Problem. The milk had been delivered, but the post was late, so there were only the milkman's footprints on the drive, coming and going. Liney might be crazy, but she wasn't stupid. When she concluded that Alaric had gone out while she was in the garage, she would expect to see a second set of prints leading away from the house. He considered running across the garden and creating the extra footprints, but decided against it when he couldn't think of a way of getting back without leaving return prints. He'd have to chance it.

Back in his room, he closed the door and placed his hands on the glass dome. He gritted his teeth. These trips were no joyrides. If smoking could damage your health, what the hell could a heart-and-lung-crushing trip to an alternate reality do? But he had to go. Things to sort out. He concentrated on the model house, steeling himself for the coming agony. When it didn't happen, he realized that he had no more idea how to use the thing after three excursions than he had before the first. Even last night, when he'd been so furious about Naia's housekeeping efforts, he hadn't known what to do. But the pain had overtaken him anyway, and kicked him into the garden, and that was all he cared about at the time. So what did he do then that he wasn't doing now?

"On those three occasions were you upset in any way? I mean angry, sad, particularly emotional?"

He'd dodged the question when she'd asked it. None

of her business how he was feeling. But could she be on to something? He thought back. Just before the first trip he'd been longing, really longing, for Withern as it used to be, before Mum died. The second time he'd been yearning to revisit the alternate version of the house discovered the day before. And last night? He'd been in a real state. Absolutely furious. So . . .

With his hands on the dome, he tried tapping into his emotions. Tried to dredge up a longing for Naia's Withern. No result. He tried to make himself angry, but what little anger he managed proved as inadequate as the feigned longing. He made a couple of other attempts, but the nearest he could get to any real passion was frustration, and frustration obviously wasn't a driving force. He gave up.

5.2

Naia spent half the morning in her room in case Alaric came. He wasn't obliged to come, and they'd made no definite arrangement, but she didn't see how he could bear to stay away with so much still to work out. She gave up waiting around eleven but couldn't settle downstairs and continually visited her room in case he'd turned up in her absence.

"You like it up there, don't you?" her mother said after one of these brief returns.

"It's my room," she replied. "Shouldn't I?"

Alex thought she had a pretty good idea why Naia was so restless. She was expecting a call from that boy she was keen on. Robert. She'd seen a photo of him. Nice-looking lad, dark curly hair with blue tips, bright smile, starting at art college in September. What she didn't know, because Naia hadn't told her, was that Robert was away this week, visiting grandparents in Bristol. His grandmother had just learned that she had liver cancer and was unlikely to see the end of the year.

Ordinarily, Naia might have missed Robert. They'd been getting closer lately. Bit too free with his hands, but that was boys for you. She spent hours talking to him on the phone behind closed doors. However, he'd hardly crossed her mind since Alaric had appeared on the scene. There was no betrayal in this. She wasn't attracted to Alaric. Appalling idea. It would be like fancying a brother who'd been away all her life. But she did need to see him. Why didn't he come? What was so fascinating at that dismal Withern of his that could keep him from her and the world of knowledge and speculation that they'd only just begun to explore?

5.3

It was a single garage with a gray slate roof in keeping with the house roofs, though it had been built many years after the house, for the first car owned by the Underwoods then at Withern Rise. Alaric peered into shadows that smelled of dust and oil. Strange to see Liney's little green Fiat there instead of Dad's old blue Daimler. The Daimler had been in the family from new; Alaric's grandfather had bought it to celebrate the birth of his son, never dreaming that it would still be on the road forty years later—driven by that same son.

"Hello?"

"Up here!"

At the dim far end of the garage, a steep open-sided staircase climbed to the storage space under the eaves. Reaching a standing position at the top, Alaric was forced into an uncomfortable stoop. Even as its highest point the roof's inverted V was so low that no one approaching average height could hope to stand upright. He couldn't and Liney couldn't. When he last had come up here with his mother, she had been able to stand upright and he had stood on tiptoe in the middle. He'd never thought of it before, but Mum hadn't been that tall.

"Thought you were going out," Liney said.

"Changed my mind. I'll go later. Or tomorrow."

He watched her rooting through boxes, lifting cans of paint to inspect the color on the label or around the rim, in the fragment of gray light admitted by the skylight. There were many other things up here as well as paint—pieces of old furniture, a roll of coconut matting, some musty carpet scraps, various bits of junk that should have been chucked out years ago. In the gloom Alaric picked out the rusty tricycle he'd careered on around the garden until the age of four; boxes of games and puzzles; his old orange football. There were also a great many picture frames. His mother had collected frames the way other people collect stamps or snuffboxes or thimbles. If she saw one she liked and it was in fair condition and reasonably priced, she bought it. Only a percentage of her frames had ever been allocated pictures and hung in the house, but he remembered her saying that one day she would find a picture and a place for every one of them. She hadn't, of course. There hadn't been time.

"Which room should we tackle first?" Liney asked him. "Which room, which color?"

"Not bothered," he replied.

"Come on, Alaric, input, input. It's too cold to crouch up here all day." He looked through the cans, but remained unable to commit his interest to any of them, or any room. "All right, I'll choose," Liney said in exasperation. "This one, and we'll do the kitchen because it's the warmest while the heating's out of action."

The color she'd picked for the kitchen was a faint yellow called Morning Mist.

"How boring can you get?" Alaric said.

"You can still choose. Your house."

"It'll do. It's only the kitchen."

A large walk-in pantry attached to the kitchen was an all-purpose utility room these days. This cold room, never heated, contained a washing machine, a dryer, an immense freezer that grumbled and juddered, and a substantial enamel sink in which Liney placed some stiff brushes in bowls of turpentine. She asked Alaric to spread newspaper over the kitchen floor so they wouldn't drop paint on it.

"Probably improve that floor," he said.

"Maybe it would, but we're painting the walls, not the floor."

"What do I do for newspaper?"

"Try the front step."

He fetched a couple of the bags from the step and commenced to lay sheets of newspaper from them on the floor.

"Filthy," Liney said suddenly. She was looking at a licked finger she'd run down the wall. "Have to wipe them over first."

"Your fingers?"

"The walls."

"Oh, that'll take ages."

"No, it won't. I'm a whirlwind once I get going."

She filled a plastic bucket with hot soapy water and began swabbing the walls down with one of two big yellow car sponges she'd found under the sink. She told Alaric to grab the second sponge and follow her example. He fell into a brooding silence but set to work.

Liney proved a whirlwind indeed, finishing three walls before he'd done one. "Brighter already," she said, admiring their handiwork.

"Don't really need to paint now, do we?" he said hopefully.

"Yes, we do, you're not getting out of it that easily."

He scowled. "Didn't know I was being *forced* to help."

"You're not," Liney said. "You're under no obligation at all. I, however, will do my best in the time available to improve your home. And when I've done what I can, I shall return to my lonely, spinsterish flat in Sheringham, knowing that my endeavors have gone quite unappreciated by the work-shy men of this household."

"I was kidding," he said lamely.

She flashed him a fake smile. "So was I. Now let's get cracking, shall we?"

5.4

When Mr. Dukas, the heating engineer, still hadn't arrived by twelve, Liney rang his number. His wife answered and informed her that Jim was out on a job.

"Not this job," Liney said, and asked if Jim had any plans to visit Withern Rise as agreed.

"Hang on, I'll look in the book." Liney heard pages being turned and finally: "Nothing here."

"What do you mean, nothing there?"

"No mention of an appointment at Withern Rise."

"But I arranged it with him yesterday. He was coming here to work out an estimate for central heating repairs."

"Ah, yesterday," Mrs. Dukas said. "I was visiting my mother at the home yesterday."

"Is that . . . relevant?"

"Sorry?"

"I mean, do you have to be there when your husband makes appointments?"

"It helps. Jim never writes things down, see. Trusts to memory."

"Perhaps he shouldn't," Liney said.

"You're right, I'm always telling him that. Like a sieve, his."

The amiable Mrs. Dukas promised to phone her husband immediately on his mobile and ask him to look in on Withern before he came home. Liney waited until half past six before ringing back. This time the man himself answered. Yes, he had forgotten the original arrangement, he confessed, and his wife had forgotten to tell him to come that afternoon.

Liney asked him when he thought he might find the time to actually pass their way. He once again promised to be there first thing in the morning, eight thirty sharp.

"Will you put it in the book to make sure?" Liney asked.

"I'll get the wife to do it," he replied.

_____ Day Four

4.1

Mr. Dukas was almost as good as his latest word. He didn't make the eight-thirty appointment next morning, but he was there on the dot of five past one. Alaric and Liney were sitting down to a bread-and-cheese lunch.

"We've earned this," Liney said, gazing about her at the freshly painted kitchen.

"Yep," Alaric said. "Hard bread and old cheese seem a fair reward."

When the doorbell rang, Liney kicked back her chair and ran into the hall. She drew the door back so sharply that the man on the step almost had a coronary among the cardboard boxes. He was a broad man in his forties with a narrow head topped with an island of matted ginger hair. He wore dark blue overalls, too short for him in leg and arm, and carried a large green metal box that looked as if it had been ritually abused with a metal toe cap at least three times a week for two decades. When Mr. Dukas finally crossed the threshold, he shivered. "Chilly in here."

"Yes," Liney said. "We really ought to call a heating engineer."

He asked to see the boiler. Liney led him into the kitchen, where Alaric was still eating. She announced him like a crown prince of Europe.

"Mr. Dukas is among us!"

She showed him through to the utility room, where he removed the front panel of the boiler and got down on his blue knees before it.

"Old boiler," he said, tapping a few things with a wrench.

"No need to be personal," Liney said.

It didn't take him long to find out what was wrong. A valve had expired. Liney asked him if he could replace it. Mr. Dukas said he doubted it, as they didn't make them anymore.

"Well, what are we supposed to do?"

"Get a new boiler, that's my advice."

"Wouldn't that be expensive?" Liney asked.

"Wouldn't be cheap."

"Are you sure you can't get a new valve to replace the old?"

"There *might* still be the odd one about," Mr. Dukas opined. "Long shot, though."

"Could you find out?"

He unclipped his phone from his belt, pressed buttons, put the phone to his ear, and waited. Then he asked after the health of the person who had picked up, quoted the number of the valve, and waited while the person at the other end ran a check of his stock and suppliers. When the call was concluded, Mr. Dukas turned to Liney.

"Nope. Obsolete, see."

"So . . . that's it?"

"Just about."

"You're absolutely sure this valve is unobtainable?"

"That's what Mario said."

"Mario? You asked a waiter?" Mr. Dukas looked puzzled. "Sorry," Liney said. "This Mario. He's an expert in things valvish, is he? I mean, he's the main man to go to with one's valve problems?"

"If Mario can't get it, it doesn't exist."

"I see. But I was wondering if there were others who might perhaps have a biscuit tin chockablock with obsolete valves."

"Biscuit tin?"

"Or some such. You never know."

Mr. Dukas mused. "Well, there's old Blathering . . . "

"Blathering?"

"Reg Blathering. Used to have an ironmonger's in Stone. You could buy a single nail from old Reg."

"Do you think a single nail would do the trick?"

"I mean he used to stock all sorts of odds and sods that no one else would bother with. If you couldn't get what you wanted from the big boys, you'd go to Reg Blathering and nine times out of ten he'd have it."

"He *used* to have a shop, you say?"

Mr. Dukas nodded. "Up to about ten years ago. Then he retired. But he still has most of his unsold stock. Garage full of it. I've had a fair few bits and pieces off him over the years."

"And you think he might have one of these obsolete valves we need?"

"Highly unlikely. But I could pop along and ask."

"Couldn't you phone him? You can use ours."

Mr. Dukas shook his head. "He's not on it. I remember him saying he had it taken out because the bloody thing kept ringing. I'll go see him personally."

When he'd gone, Liney sighed. "Well, that's the last we'll hear from *him.*"

4.2

For Naia, yesterday had seemed endless. Barely a third over, today was also dragging. Where was Alaric? Why didn't he come? How long was she expected to wait for him? Three friends had phoned to invite her to mess around in the snow, and each time she'd made excuses. A heavy period was the one they most readily understood. Her mother, overhearing this as she passed on one occasion, murmured: "I'm saying *nothing.*"

By one o'clock she was seriously thinking of saying to hell with Alaric Underwood and going out anyway. When Alex asked her if she fancied going for a walk, she accepted, hoping the friends she'd put off wouldn't see her.

4.3

Alaric made his excuses, donned his outdoor things, pretended to go out the front door, and sneaked up to his room. There, moving more quietly than most mice, he crouched over the Folly with his hands around the dome. After yesterday's failure he wasn't at all certain of success, but he had to try. A second failure would mean once again having to tell Liney that he'd changed his mind about going out and, again, feeling obliged to help with the sodding DIY. He concentrated his emotional energies, such as he could muster, hoping they would be sufficient, but five minutes later he was still there. He became despondent and only then noticed that the reflection in the dome wasn't as it should be. He glanced at the window. It had stopped snowing.

He sat back on the arm of the chair. If snowfall was one of the factors that activated the Folly and they'd had all they were going to get, there might be no more visits until next winter. And suppose there wasn't any snow then? Who knew when he'd be able to return to the other reality, or see Naia, or . . .

Or her mother. That was really what it was about. Who. The other Alex Underwood. All yesterday and this morning while working with Liney she'd never been far from his thoughts. The woman he'd grieved for and missed so desperately for so long was still alive, elsewhere. He'd heard her voice, and if he had stepped out onto Naia's landing and looked down he would have seen her at the bottom of the stairs. So close. He stretched out a finger and ran it lightly down the glass of the Folly, wishing he could look the other Alex in the eye, see that quick smile of hers, touch her hand—

The tingling was so short-lived that he had no time to prepare for the pain that shot up his arm, blasted his insides, and sent him reeling to the floor. Perhaps because the route was now established, the room vanished quickly, and at once he was lying in the snow under the tree, the agony subsiding.

"Where did you spring from?"

Naia: bounding across the garden toward him. She ran like Liney, the aunt she didn't have, arms and legs all over the place.

He sat up. "Take a wild guess."

"But it's stopped snowing!"

"Well, that's one factor less." How nice for you that it's the only one I came up with, he thought.

She drew near. "So we're not locked into the season or the climate. We can go on seeing each other all through the year."

"Yippee," he said in a flat voice.

She stopped in front of him, looking down. "Where

have you been? I thought you'd have come before this."

His chest ached and he felt as if his insides were shaking. He wanted only to sit quietly until it all went away, but he started to get up because Naia was there, waiting.

"I was busy."

She reached down to help. He would have shrugged her off, but she was too quick, and as she gripped his arm an intense shock ripped through them: both of them. They fell back as though kicked.

"What was *that?*"

"It was like an electric current!"

"Feels like my hair's standing on end."

Alaric scrambled to his feet. He reached for her. She jumped back.

"What are you doing?"

"Need to see if it'll happen again."

"Not on your life."

"We have to. It's never happened before. Why this time?"

He started forward and grabbed her arm before she

could put more space between them. In the instant of contact, the current raced through them, twitching every part of them. They would have flown apart this time too, but Alaric held on tight.

"Let go!" Naia cried. "Let go, it's killing me!"

He didn't let go. Agonizing as it was, for him as well as her, he needed to see if anything else would happen. Something did. As the shock continued to course through them his hand sank into the material of her coat, into her arm. Even in their agony, they stared in horror as his hand met a point of resistance. To him it felt like gripping a tube of foam rubber, while Naia, on the receiving end, felt his hand enclosing the bone. She tore her arm out of his grip. The current died.

"That was horrible!" she said. "Disgusting! What was it?"

"Don't know, but there has to be a reason for it. What are we doing this time that's so different?"

"Only difference I can think of is that we were indoors before."

"Can't be that," he said. "Too simple."

"Who says it has to be complicated? Have you been inside yet? I mean this time, today?"

"Didn't get a chance. You came lumbering up just as I got here."

"That's it then. You haven't arrived properly yet."

"Eh?"

She took a jagged breath, still quivering all over from the shock, as was he.

"Your Folly sends you to my reality, and mine sends me to yours, and we have to stop off in the garden on the way, yours or mine, depending on which of us is making the trip. God, I think it's wearing off. The gardens are sort of changeover points. You won't be fully integrated into my reality until my Folly receives you. You have to finish the journey."

"What about the shocks?"

"I would guess that we can't coexist at the halfway points. Nature's way of pointing this out. The pain when we set out is probably another hint that we're defying a physical law or two. I mean, if it was normal or easy everyone would be at it, wouldn't they? We'd be taking holidays on alternate beaches because they're cleaner than ours or have fewer nudists or something."

"Or more," Alaric said. He glanced at the house. "Where's your mum?"

"Don't worry, she's gone walkies. I was going too, but I turned back, thought I'd better stick around in case you . . . Where are you going?"

He'd set off toward the house. "Where'd you think?"

She ran after him, boots sinking into the snow.

"Wait. Stop. You can't get in that way."

"Why, is it locked?"

"Yes. I told you, I was going out. Saw you before I had a chance to unlock it. But that's not the—"

He stopped. Held out his hand as she caught up with him.

"Key."

"What are you," she said, "some sort of masochist?"

He lowered his hand. "Drop it on the ground then."

She didn't drop the key on the ground. She said: "You cannot go in by the *door*. It won't *work* that way. You should know that better than anyone."

She was right, of course. Wasn't she always? Annoyed, he turned his back on her, glared at the house, imagined himself inside it. That was all it took. All it had ever taken, and he'd forgotten. Pea brain.

Naia watched him fade. Soon all that was left to show that he'd been there were his footprints—very shallow compared to hers—which would not continue beyond this point. He's inside, she thought. Up in my room. Ruining my carpet.

4.4

It was the first time he'd been alone in Naia's house and he wanted to make the most of it. But he had to get a move on. If he took too long she'd probably come looking for him; or worse, her mother might return and find him prowling about. Much as he wanted to see the Alex Underwood of this reality, it was not as an assumed intruder. He removed his snow-encrusted boots in Naia's room and hurried along the landing carrying them, glancing into one room after another. The most noteworthy were the bathroom—snazzy new fixtures, Jacuzzi, power shower—and the master bedroom. The bedroom looked much as his parents' room had when Mum was alive, but even brighter and fresher than he remembered. It was hard to imagine this room littered with overflowing ashtrays and stray shoes, the pillows and duvet anything less than pristine, junk on the marble dresser. When he opened the right-hand side of the wardrobe, he found it full of clothes, Alex Underwood's clothes, as that half of his parents' wardrobe had once been.

He headed down the broad staircase. Like the bedrooms and the landing, the stairs had been recarpeted. He paused halfway, on the platform that divided the upper flight from the lower. Just stood there, soaking it up. All about him, above and below, the house glowed with light and life and warmth. He'd forgotten it could be like this.

Reaching the lower hall, he turned left, into the Long Room. He used to love this room at home, with its French windows opening onto the great spread of the south garden. These days it was merely a place to flop and watch TV. There was never a fire in the grate, as there was here. Like the rest of the house, this room had been redecorated quite recently, and there were a number of new furnishings. At the far end, where logs spat and crackled behind an antique fireguard, he found a large plasma TV and a substantial new couch and armchairs.

He was about to leave the room when he saw the guitar. A Spanish acoustic of moderate quality, it leaned casually against the wall as if set down moments before. His mother's guitar, identical to this, had long since been confined to the attic with those others of her things that hadn't been sold, given away, or destroyed. Running a finger across the strings, Alaric imagined her playing quietly to herself, as she so often had when believing herself unobserved, unheard. Well, sort of playing. The guitar was one of the few things Alex had attempted and failed to master. Perhaps if she'd taken lessons she might have made more progress, but she liked to be self-taught in all things. She'd managed to pick up the basic chords, and a few more complex ones, but technique of any standard had eluded her.

Alaric recalled mocking her efforts to her face, but he'd enjoyed hearing her plunking away at the strings in her forlorn pursuit of competence, somewhere in the house. Sometimes she would sing along, with a wavering, uncertain voice, to her elementary strumming or clumsy finger picking. She was as poor a vocalist as she was a musician, yet for Alaric these things had been part of her. They'd been his mother.

He crossed the hall to the kitchen, where he found the shoddy curtains replaced by elegant roller blinds, the greasy old range turned into a multiburner gas stove, and a big new sink with shiny taps and double drainers, custom-built units below. The brittle old vinyl had been torn up, the boards underneath stripped and varnished. Even the pots and pans he'd last seen burned and blackened shined here, or had been replaced. Gleaming copper bowls and pots and utensils hung on hooks from the ceiling. There were shelves of recipe books, an expensive bread maker, a new microwave, and on the walls lots of kitcheny pictures, charts, and memo pads. It was all so neat and bright and decently used. His and Liney's efforts seemed feeble by comparison. The only remotely pleasing observation he could make was that the walls appeared to be the very color they'd chosen for his kitchen.

Withern Rise was the only home Alaric had ever known, so it did not seem exceptional to him; but with its tall chimneys, its enormous garden and river frontage, it was the sort of property usually occupied by moneyed folk. The Underwoods of this generation and the last were far from wealthy. If Alaric's parents had been burdened with a hefty mortgage, they would have been in some difficulty much of the time. They'd always worked, but his mother had only been modestly paid, and Dad's business had rarely done much more than break even. There'd never been enough in the kitty for the sort of showy extras the owners of such properties seem to treat themselves to as a matter of course. Alaric imagined that things had always been much the same for Naia's family. But all this new stuff. All the work that had been done here. Where had the money come from?

Returning to the hall, he stood with his back to the front door, gazing down the long shiny hallway, with its polished woodwork, little side tables just so, a vase of lilies on one of them. A terrible sadness welled up in him. This was the Withern Rise he would have known if his mother had lived. The house he would have come home to from school, woken up to, invited friends into. The home he would have taken for granted if his and Naia's lives had been reversed.

4.5

Naia didn't expect her mother back yet, but she thought it best to stand guard outside just in case. She had unlocked the front door and given Alaric what seemed an eternity, and she was about to go in and shout for him when the door opened and he stood there frowning, like the irritated owner preparing to dismiss the latest itinerant vacuum salesman.

"What kept you?"

He sat down to pull his boots on. "I didn't know there was a time limit."

She touched his shoulder. "No shock. No give. Which confirms it. We can coexist in the same reality only when we've reached the other person's Folly."

He got up, shoved past her, walked away from the house.

"You're not going out?" she said, pulling the door to.

"What's it to you?"

"You can't."

He flung himself around—"Why not? Because I don't *belong* here?"—and stormed off toward the side gate.

Ordinarily he would have stuck to the paths that swung around the northern section of the garden, but with the paths concealed, he walked as if they'd never existed. Trailing approximately in his wake, Naia stuck to where she knew the paths to be, following her mother's tracks between the kitchen garden (which was nowhere near the kitchen) and the wall that separated Withern from the old cemetery.

Alaric was almost at the gate when he heard a tiny

ringing sound. A young white cat had jumped down from the wall and was picking its way toward him, lifting each paw in turn clear of the snow.

"Yours, I suppose?" he said to Naia, some way behind.

Naia hadn't heard the bell or, it being white on white, noticed the cat. "Mine? What?" But then she saw it. "Oh. No. Must be a neighbor's."

The cat reached Alaric as he was about to open the gate and wound itself around his ankles. He stooped to pry it loose. The little creature raised its head in hope of a tickle under the chin. The bell around its neck jingled brightly. As he administered the requisite tickle, he saw its name on the collar. He looked closer. The cat's name was Alaric. "Oh, hilarious!" he said, pushing the animal away. It squealed and sped off, skimming the surface of the snow, while its human namesake tore the gate back, went through it, slammed it behind him.

Naia had no idea what he'd meant about the cat or why he was so angry, but when he shut the gate on her she had no problem letting it stay shut. She could do without him in that sort of mood.

In the lane beyond the gate, Alaric had a choice of just two directions. If he turned right he would pass his old primary school and enter the main street. There were four shops in his village: a newsagent's, a bicycle repair shop, a small supermarket, and an art supply shop. There were also two pubs and a Chinese takeaway. Curious as he was to see if everything was exactly the same, he worried that he might bump into people he recognized—people who might know of an Underwood daughter but would know nothing of an Underwood son. He turned left.

The six-foot-high garden wall ran all the way to the river. Some months earlier a section of it—of both this wall and Alaric's—had fallen in, or been pushed in, allowing strollers to see into the garden. Naia's wall, unlike his, had been repaired.

As he walked, Alaric was struck by how quiet it was. The snow slowed muffled all sound. Everything felt unreal, unused, uninhabited. It was as if the everyday world had twisted just out of reach. It had, in a way. A light snow began to fall once more as he reached the river, where the wall's final pillar was concreted into the bank. Standing there, lost in the stillness, his anger drained away. The river had always been a great soother for him. It was now a broad white sheet that stretched without a single crease to the opposite bank, with its unruly thicket of winter trees and scrub, wild grasses, frozen reeds, bulrushes. With the snow concealing so much, there was no noticeable difference between this view and his own. The only differences he knew about were personal. Standing there, he decided that he must confront the most profound of these differences. Immediately.

He turned from the river, headed back the way he'd come. He was just passing the gate in the wall when a black-coated figure descended the cemetery steps some fifteen yards on and started toward him. He was elderly, thin, rather frail looking, and he walked oddly, like a young boy trying to act the part of someone getting on in years. Alaric remembered him at once: the loiterer gazing at the house from across the river the day all this started. But that was in his reality, not Naia's. This version of the man might never have stood on the opposite bank or given Withern Rise a moment's attention or thought.

He pulled his hood up and retreated into it, like a tortoise into its shell. The two approached each other, two pairs of feet scuffing silence. They were about to pass when the man cleared his throat, compelling Alaric to glance his way in spite of his intention to avoid eye contact. The man was staring at him. Staring with eyes surprisingly wide and unworldly for some-one his age, as though they'd seen a great deal less of life than they surely had. There was something in that stare that made Alaric uneasy. The unease was not alle-viated by the words he heard as the man passed: "I'm the only one left," uttered in a curiously light, youth-ful voice thickened more by regret than by age.

When he reached the cemetery steps, Alaric glanced back to make sure he wasn't being pursued by the mad axman of Eynesford. The fellow seemed to have forgotten him. He was standing on tiptoe, trying to see over the wall into Withern's garden.

4.6

Naia did not go back to the house. She was fed up of being indoors. There wasn't even anyone to talk to there. But she couldn't leave the garden now either. She would have to lock the door, and if she locked the door Alaric wouldn't be able to get in, which meant he would be unable to reach the Folly in her room and go home.

Before her lay the south garden. Old photos showed that there were once extensive flower beds here, and an apple tree and a pear. In one picture, taken in the early 1940s when Grandpa Rayner was little, a string hammock hung between the two trees. Both fruit trees, along with the flower beds, had been removed by the non-Underwoods who lived there from 1947 to '63. The Family Tree had survived only because it wasn't in the way of the tennis court they wanted to put there. Luckily they'd opted for a grass court, but no one had played tennis here for decades, so this part of the garden had ended up as nothing more than an empty lawn with that single huge tree. The smooth whiteness of the snow all the way up to and around the old oak's trunk was disrupted only by the marks she and Alaric had made following his arrival and the elongated lump of the bough that had snapped off some weeks ago. Naia sat down on the bough, dug her hands into her pockets, and for want of a more exhilarating subject, tried to find some justification for Alaric's boorishness.

He'd had a rough time of it. Mother taken from him in the most grotesque way imaginable, then two years of despair and declining fortunes. She wouldn't mind betting he'd lost some friends, too. Who needs the company of such a misery? And his schoolwork had probably suffered. Bad reports about his work and attitude seemed inevitable. She chided herself. How shallow of her to expect him to be an easy companion. He'd lost everything and seen for himself that she'd lost nothing. Quite the reverse. Oh. Of course. *That* was why he was in such a foul mood when he came out of the house. Her home was a palace compared to his. The differences must have really hurt. Just as well she hadn't told him about the Lotto win. They didn't often buy a ticket, the odds being so stacked, but about a year ago, on impulse, Mum had picked one up at the newsagent's—and her numbers had come up. It wasn't one of those massive multimillion jackpot wins, but it had paid for a stack of new furniture and carpets, curtains, a decent bathroom and kitchen, and the Saab (three years old, but an infant compared to the ancient Daimler). They'd also had much of the house professionally decorated for the first time ever. There'd been no such improvements or additions at Alaric's. There'd been no Lotto win. No Alex to buy the ticket.

4.7

Alaric climbed the five long shallow steps up from the lane and paused at the top. The little graveyard, dotted with yews, holly trees, and slabs of standing snow, fanned out before him. He knew where he had to go, but now that he was here he found that he needed to work up to the moment of incontrovertible truth; so he avoided that place, looked anywhere but. Halfway along the concealed path that ran from one end of the cemetery to the other, he came to a notice mounted on a wooden post. He'd seen no such notice in his cemetery, but he hadn't been there for a month or two and it looked fairly new. There were drawings on it—commissioned drawings, not graffiti (for the moment)—of garden birds, butterflies, frogs, wildflowers. At the top were the words:

EYNESFORD OLD CEMETERY

Below this was the information that it was now a conservation site, where no further burials would be permitted. And . . .

> *Eynesford Old Cemetery is now being cared for in an environmentally friendly manner that will benefit wildlife. The*

grass will be cut only in early and late summer to create conditions for a range of plants to grow. Over the next few years, as the area becomes more established, visitors can expect to see an increasing variety and quantity of herbs and wildflowers. These plants will provide an important food source for birds and insects.

Alaric stepped off the path and ambled between the stones and monuments. Some of them had been badly vandalized, the same ones, he was sure, that had been vandalized at home—most likely by alternate versions of the same vandals. Born twice, given two shots at life, and in both realities they chose to destroy and deface for the sake of it. Many of the graves were bunched together, but others were well spaced out. There was plenty of room for new graves without overcrowding. But he was glad there'd be no more. Mum always said she liked room to—

Fool! She wasn't buried here. Wasn't *dead* here. He marched to the wall that separated the cemetery from the house. Other footprints preceded his, but he paid these no mind. The wall, battered by time and the elements, supported a thick cloak of ivy, but its height was currently increased further still by three days' snow. He came to a particular spot, beyond which, on the other side of the wall, a gable end rose steeply, the smoke from its chimney fragmented by the dancing snow. So easy to imagine that it was his house there, and that two Februaries ago, on a day much like this, a small group of mourners had assembled at a precise equivalent of this spot to bury his mother.

Even now his chest heaved at the thought. He would never forget the lowering of that hideous box into the neat snowrimmed hole in the ground. The funeral, following so swiftly on from her death, had numbed him so much that it wasn't until some weeks later that he had thought to ask his father why he had opted for a church service, with all the religious flummery he despised, before incarcerating her in so-called consecrated ground. "It seemed the thing to do," Ivan had replied. "And why here? Because she loved this place. Withern, I mean, not the boneyard. Thought she'd have wanted to remain as close as could be managed . . . "

Alaric allowed his gaze to drop at last to the base of the wall, where he saw to his surprise a headstone like his mother's within a shallow cloister of ivy. What was this? If she hadn't died in this reality, if they hadn't buried her here, why the same stone? Whose grave could this be? The ivy drooped over the top third of the stone so that he couldn't make out the words etched into it until he dropped into a crouch and craned forward. Then he saw that in spite of the similarity it was a considerably older stone than his mother's. Someone had recently cleared the snow from the inscription, but he gave this no thought as he read:

ALDOUS UNDERWOOD

BELOVED SON AND BROTHER

1934–1945

Aldous? Wasn't that the name of the horny bishop Naia had told him about? The builder of Withern Rise? This was the grave of a much later Aldous Underwood, but he was struck by the coincidence of coming across such an uncommon name two days' running. He pondered the dates of birth and death on the stone. Just a kid when he snuffed it. "Beloved son and brother." Whose son? Whose brother? He must have been Grandpa Rayner's generation. Would Dad know of him? Maybe. Unless . . . and it was certainly a possibility . . . unless he hadn't been born at all in their reality.

Well, what did it matter now? History. The main thing was, he'd gotten what he came for: absolute proof that there was no Alex Underwood buried here. That the voice he'd heard calling in Naia's house really had belonged to her. That the photo in the little wallet had not been some sort of . . .

Crunch of snow behind him. His already cold spine froze utterly. Even in broad daylight a graveyard isn't a place you want to hear unexpected footsteps. He turned, hoping it was Naia.

"Hello," said Alex Underwood.

She stood smiling at him from the foot of the grave. He withdrew at once into the shadow of his hood and snapped his chin down hard.

"I didn't expect to find anyone else here, day like this," she said.

His heart was thumping so hard it was a wonder she didn't hear it. He couldn't speak. Couldn't even grunt. But then she said something that shook him almost as much as finding her standing behind him.

"This is my spot."

Her spot? She knew that? But how? Surely she didn't know about his reality, his Withern Rise, the alternate version of herself who . . .

She must have realized how it had sounded, for she gave a small laugh and said. "I cut through here all the time, and I'm often drawn to this little corner, don't ask me why. I didn't know him, obviously. You?"

"Me?" From his lowered hood.

"I mean why are you here—if you don't mind my asking?"

"I'm not a vandal," he said defensively.

"I didn't take you for one." She moved forward to the other side of the grave. "Poor lad," she said sadly.

He raised his head a little, assuming she was referring to him. She was looking down at the gravestone, which gave him a chance to study her. She wore a green head scarf, from which a fringe of snow-frosted fair hair jutted. There was a small crease between her eyes. He'd forgotten that crease. It used to appear at all sorts of odd moments: when she was stressed or elated, thoughtful or angry. There was more strain in her face than he remembered, but time had passed, and she had had that near-death experience. How often he'd dreamed a situation like this, in which she'd come back to him, only to wake and find himself as bereft and lonely as ever. But here she was, here she definitely was, no dream, standing by the grave he'd seen her lowered into two years earlier. He was torn between running in horror from the cemetery and leaping over the grave and flinging his arms around her, covering her face with kisses. Before he was quite driven to either course, she spoke again.

"So young. I can't imagine how I would cope with such a loss. Killed his father, you know."

Alaric pulled himself together. "Killed his . . . ?"

"The boy's death. And with her son and husband gone, Mrs. Underwood sold up and moved away with her surviving children. I think I might have done the same. I *think*. Could I really leave a child of mine here all alone? Not sure, to be honest."

She looked up without warning, saw him full face for the first time. And staggered.

"But you . . . you're the image of . . . "

Her eyes flitted across his face as she struggled to make sense of the impossible likeness between this stranger and her daughter. He no longer shrank from her examination, but then it came to him that if he stayed there much longer she would understand everything, thanks either to some innate sixth sense or his inability to keep his mouth shut. He mumbled something about having to go and turned away.

"No, wait."

She hastened around the grave, headed him off. She was within arm's reach of him. Don't touch me, he thought. I don't know what I'll do if you touch me.

"Do you live around here?" she asked. "I've never seen you. I would have remembered if I'd seen you."

She imposed the very slightest emphasis on the last "you."

"Visiting," he mumbled, with some truth.

"Who?"

"What?"

"Who are you visiting? Who are you staying w—" She checked herself. "Sorry, none of my business." And, rather too casually: "Which way are you going?"

He nodded toward the second exit, at the southern end of the cemetery.

"Me, too," she said.

They stumbled through the snow-thick grass to the path. He was surprised to find that he was much taller than her now; also that she limped slightly. Had she hurt her leg in the crash? Naia hadn't mentioned that. But even with her unsmooth stride, he felt lumpen walking beside her, ungainly, self-conscious, foolish.

She talked nonstop about inconsequentials—the weather, the condition of the graves, something on the news—as if her sanity depended on not pausing to think or consider. The tremor in her voice was impossible to miss. Nerves. He made her nervous. If she only knew what state she put *him* into! He felt obliged to make the odd comment or observation, but his voice was harsh and immature in his ears, his words poorly formed, enunciated, strung together. What a clod. Nevertheless, he was barely able to conceal his joy at this unexpected turn of events, and he let his hood slip back a little so that she could see him more clearly still. His concern that everything would suddenly click into place for her, that a flash of intuition would unmask him, had evaporated. The exhilaration of being here with her far outweighed such fears. Every so often he cast a sly glance her way, hoping to meet her eye through the tumbling snow. Once, succeeding, her amazement again broke through.

"It's unbelievable. You're so much like my Naia, you

might be my . . . " She bit the last word off just in time.

The cemetery ended about halfway along the wall that defined the eastern boundary of Withern Rise. The path, now bordered on both sides by unoccupied ground topped with whitened turf, continued until it met a tarmac road. Until twenty-odd years ago this road had been a simple track down to a favorite riverside spot for picnicking families, but in the mid-1980s a swathe of common land bounded by the track was sold for development, and a number of mock Tudor houses sprang up. Alaric and Alex had almost reached the road when two women rounded the corner. He knew both women by sight. They didn't know him, of course, not here, though one of them blinked with surprise on seeing him: that likeness again. They greeted Alex, and when she stopped to exchange a few words, he said, "See you," and hurried on ahead.

Reaching the road, he glanced back. She was talking to the women, but he felt she must have been watching him, because she waved to him over their shoulders. He raised his hand in return and passed beyond her sight behind the dense bushes between the path's end and the five-bar gate at the head of Withern's drive. The gate stood open, as it always did at home. Same gate, except this one didn't have a broken strut. He started along the drive. The occasional gap in the trees and bushes on his left allowed a clear view of the house. When Alex parted company with the women she too would come this way, and easily see him if he wasn't inside the house by then. He got a move on; made it to the front step, through the door.

"Hey!" he shouted, closing the door behind him.

A movement in the Long Room to his left, and "Hey yourself," followed by Naia's head around the door.

"The Folly! Your mum's coming!"

"Oh, no!" She ran out, grabbed him by the sleeve, started hauling him along the hall.

"My boots!"

She stopped. "Get that snow off!" He stamped his feet. "On the *mat*!" she growled.

He went back, leaving a very visible trail, and

stamped hard on the doormat. Naia was waiting for him when he reached the bottom of the stairs. They started up.

"How close is she?"

"Close enough."

She caught his expression.

"Chirpy all of a sudden, aren't we?"

"Is there a law against it here?"

He beat her to the top and almost danced along the landing, glancing to left and right and all about with new eyes. Naia couldn't understand it. From that miserable state to this in such a short space of time? Why? What had happened?

She never did find out.

4.8

The first thing he heard on making it back to his room was Liney, in the distance, trying to outdo Pavarotti on "*Nessun Dorma.*" Didn't the woman know *how* to be quiet? But for once he was glad she was there. Mum's big nutty sister. His own flesh and blood. He crept downstairs, boots in hand. He had intended to rush along the hall and slam the front door loudly, then hang about just long enough to give the impression that he was removing his outdoor clothes before reporting back. But Liney wasn't in the kitchen as (for some reason) he'd expected her to be. She and Luciano were just across from the stairs in the River Room, and the door was half open. He took off along the hall in his socks, and at the front door dropped his boots beside the mat, hung his coat on the hall stand, and put his slippers on. No need to slam the door with her making all that racket. He returned the way he'd come, at a more sedate pace.

He entered the River Room to find her balanced precariously on the top rung of the stepladder, one leg floating out behind her as she stretched to reach a difficult scrap of wall. She was using a roller this time, running it back and forth and up and down and anywhere she felt like over the old wallpaper. The color she'd chosen could have been worse, which was just as well, as her face and clothes were liberally spattered with it.

Sensing that she was no longer alone, Liney squawked and came close to toppling off the ladder. Alaric rushed forward and steadied it and her just in time.

"You weren't long!" she shouted.

He cupped his ear, competing with the suddenly solo Pavarotti. "What?"

"I said you weren't long!"

"Can't hear you! Turn the radio down!"

"What?" Liney bawled.

"Turn the *radio* down!"

"Can't hear you! I'll turn the radio down!"

The small digital radio with the big sound dangled from a hook near the top of the ladder. She reduced the volume.

"That's better," they said together.

"I thought you'd be gone all afternoon," she said then.

"He had to go out."

"Who did?"

"The person I had to see." He looked around.

"Shouldn't you have asked before doing this?"

"You weren't here," she said.

"I mean Dad."

"Not here either."

"There's always the phone."

"I daresay he'll ring tonight. I might ask him then."

"Bit late then."

"Well, c'est la vie." She climbed down the ladder, all flat feet and sticky-out elbows. "Good news. Mr. Dukas rang to say that the old boy who used to be an ironmonger has the very valve we need for our boiler."

"Really?"

"Really. Promised faithfully to come and fit it this afternoon, which means we could be warm by teatime. And I've arranged for a team of domestics to give the place a thorough seeing to tomorrow, top to bottom."

"Team of . . . ?"

"Cleaners. They'll dust, polish, tidy, do everything I'd like to do in a fraction of the time."

"Cost a bit, won't it?"

"My treat."

Alaric noticed the length of paint-stained rag tucked into her belt. The pattern looked familiar. He flicked it. "Where'd this come from?"

"I found a bundle of old clothes in a plastic sack in the utility room. Obviously your father's best shot at clearing a few things out before Kate gets here."

"You don't think it might be a bag of washing he was thinking of seeing to when he gets back?" Alaric said.

"Washing? Your father? Nah." But she sounded doubtful.

He examined the piece of torn material more closely, and nodded. "This is the shirt Kate sent him for Christmas."

"Christmas? This Christmas just gone?"

"That's the one."

She removed the piece of shirt from her belt and held it up by two of its three corners.

"You don't think if I wash and iron it and sew it all back together . . . "

4.9

Later that afternoon, Naia went out again. Out properly this time, beyond the garden. She felt she'd earned a spot of freedom after being cooped up for so long. It was nearly dark already, and snowing heavily once more. The village being just down the lane, she went there rather than to Stone. She found only one of her friends at home, Selma Paine, but Selma was nursing a heavy cold and didn't feel like going out or even talking much.

Having done the rounds, Naia browsed in the newsagent's for a few minutes and came back the long way, past the snack shop and the rowhouses and retirement bungalows and the mock Tudors of Coneygeare Bank, to finally, like Alaric some hours earlier, pass through Withern's main gate, adding her footprints to those fast filling in along the drive.

Still in no hurry to shut herself away, she again wandered into the south garden and to the Family Tree. This time she did not sit on the fallen bough but leaned against the tree, thinking little, watching the snow fall through the early dark. Knowing that a dead person sprawled immediately below her bothered her not at all, she found. Bishop Underwood was a long time gone.

A fair portion of the garden lay behind her, stretching to the boundary ditch that had once been a stream, around which, from the river to the main gate, a tangled wood had grown up over the years. Naia had lived at Withern all her life and couldn't imagine living anywhere else. She didn't like to think about it, but in two, three, four years she would leave it to pursue her studies or make her way in whatever profession she chose. Leave she might, but she would return and, unless her parents sold up, all this would be hers one day. She didn't like to think of that either, because for her to inherit Withern Rise, her parents would have to be dead. Alaric would probably inherit his Withern, too. The question was, would he want it? It was in a very poor state, and she doubted that he had much love for it after the last two years.

But then she remembered that Kate Faraday was

moving in. Kate would make a difference. When she'd visited them, she'd fallen in love with the house, the garden, river, everything. She and Mum had similar tastes and enthusiasms, which was one of the reasons they got on so well. Alaric might not like the idea of Kate moving in, but she could turn out to be the place's savior. His too. He'd warm to her when he saw what a difference she made. He was bound to.

Pleased with this imagined happy ending, Naia pushed herself away from the tree; pushed too vigorously, for her head went back and struck a raised section of bark. She turned, perhaps to accuse the tree of assault, and met the hole in the trunk in which, when younger, she'd placed notes. The message hole, as she had always known it, measured about a foot from top to bottom, with an interior drop of a few more inches behind the swollen rim. Around the beginning of every December when she was little, she used to reach into the hole from her dad's arms and post her list of requests to Father Christmas. He had introduced her to this tried-and-tested method of communication with the old boy as his father had introduced it to him when he was small. Results for both father and daughter had proved quite effective, most years. But even after Santa was unmasked, she continued to use the message hole to post notes to herself. She didn't know it, but Alaric had done exactly the same thing. Until the age of about twelve, they had each, in their separate realities, dropped in a message (usually written with lemon juice) and a few days later reached in to discover it with feigned surprise and rush back to the house to warm the words to visibility. It was over four years since they had posted anything in either reality's message hole, but because she'd just sorted his future for him and decided that he would be all right after all, Naia reached into the hole for old times' sake. Not expecting to find anything, she yanked out her hand when she touched something cold, fearing that it was some creature that had crawled in to die. But peering into the woody darkness, she saw a flat oblong package just below the rim. She lifted out a crude envelope, made from what felt like oilskin. In the minimal light, she could just make out three words handwritten on the front:

To THE FiNDeR

She turned the envelope over and found the flap sealed with a circle of red wax impressed with a capital A. She was wondering about this, the cryptic dedication on the front, the envelope's possible contents, when her mobile rang. She fumbled for it. "Hello?" Her mother, unaware that she was only just outside, informed her that tea was ready. As Naia headed across the lawn to the house, she stuffed the envelope in her pocket. Perhaps she would show it to Mum and see what she made of it. Perhaps she wouldn't.

4.10

When Alaric's father phoned from Newcastle that evening, Liney greeted him with a winsome: "Sweetheart." After a little light conversation, mostly on her part, she asked how he felt about having the house painted.

"Painted?" he said. "You mean as in watercolor?"

"As in latex. I'm offering to decorate the place, Ivan. Some of it, anyway. I wield a fair brush and roller, in case you don't know."

There was a pause all the way from Newcastle, before: "You've started, haven't you?"

"Well you can't expect me to just sit here twiddling my thumbs while you're up there snowballing your lady love," Liney answered.

"How far have you gotten?" He sounded worried.

"We've finished the kitchen and the River Room."

"We? Who's we?"

"Alaric, who do you think?"

"Alaric's helping you?"

"He is, yes. He has quite a flair for it, as it turns out."

"Put him on, will you?"

Alaric was bent over the Escher jigsaw in the Long Room, where Liney had lit the fire, the real fire, after raking out all the cigarette butts and locating a supply

of coal and logs. He joined her in the freezing hall—
freezing still because Mr. Dukas, in spite of his promise,
had failed to come and install the valve. Liney handed
Alaric the phone but remained at his elbow, keen to
hear both sides of the conversation.

"That woman shouldn't be allowed into civilized
society," Ivan said without preamble. "Is she bollixing
the place up, Al? Come on, the truth."

"It could be worse," he said. Liney beamed at him.
Such praise!

"You're sure? You're not just saying that?"

"I'm not just saying it."

"Al, listen. Conditions are even worse here now and
no sign of a letup. Would it be all right with you if we
drag it out a bit longer, or will you be white haired if
you're stuck there with her much longer?"

"The nerve," Liney said.

Alaric changed ears. She came around to the other
side and listened there instead.

"You should see the local TV pictures," Ivan went
on. "Roads blocked, countryside dotted with aban-

doned cars. People have been found frozen to death in their vehicles."

"So you're not coming home tomorrow."

"Don't see that we have much choice. We'll make the attempt if she's getting too much for you, though."

"Too much for him?" Liney said archly. "Me?"

"She still there?" Ivan asked.

"In my pocket," Alaric said.

"Put her in the cellar and throw away the key, that's my advice."

"We don't have a cellar."

"But is it all right? You don't mind?"

"We'll manage."

"Al . . ."

"Yeah?"

"The settlement should come through soon. Be quite a bundle. We'll buy some new stuff, shall we? New sound system for you maybe, a family car from this century, few little luxuries. I think we deserve them, don't you?"

Instead of answering, he handed the receiver back to

Liney and returned to the puzzle. He sat staring at it without seeing it. The settlement. Reparation for the railway accident that had taken his mother from him. After eighteen months of investigation and demands from lawyers, the company responsible for the track at the time had finally accepted liability and announced that the victims' next of kin would receive "generous cash payments." The size of the checks would depend on the status of the injuries sustained. *Status of the injuries.* They'd actually said that. Six-figure sums had been promised to immediate relatives of the dead. Blood money. His mother had died so that he and his dad could buy some new gear. Alaric wanted none of it. He wouldn't accept a penny, or anything bought with it.

"We're in business!" Liney crowed, bouncing in. "We have the official grunt of approval to do our worst!"

He looked up from the puzzle. "Our worst?"

"A free hand to decorate as we see fit!"

"My father said that?"

"Well, not in those actual words. But as good as,

reading between the lines. I'm a whiz at that. You'd be amazed how often a person says one thing and means the absolute opposite. Quite handy sometimes."

4.11

Naia weighed the envelope from the message hole in her hands. She turned it over; considered the A impressed into the wax seal. The only people with that initial who had easy access to the tree were her mother and Alaric, but it didn't seem the sort of thing either of them would put there. So who was A? And what should she do with the thing? Open it? Why shouldn't she? To the Finder, it said on the outside. Well, that was her. So . . .

She snapped the brittle blob of hardened wax and extracted three sheets of thick paper, which she unfolded. The text they contained was not neatly word processed like most documents these days, but type-written with a rather faded black ribbon, as follows.

```
You are a go-ahead young marketing
executive. A bachelor. It is Saturday
```

morning, and you are off to do your
week's shopping. About to get into
your car, you decide to go back
and check that you locked the
door. By going back, you leave a
minute later and miss the parking
space you would have found at the
supermarket and are forced to park
in a nearby street instead. There
are parking meters in this street,
but drivers are only allowed to
leave their cars here for thirty
minutes at a time. While you are
feeding the meter, someone calls
your name. It is a friend you
haven't seen for a while. The
friend introduces you to a
neighbor of his, who he has given
a lift into town. Call the neighbor
Helen. You and Helen are mutually
attracted, but as she's married,
you part company. Or you don't.
Two possible scenarios present
themselves.

Scenario 1. Having left the friend and Helen you go to the supermarket, fill your cart, and join a queue at the checkout—a longer queue than the one you would have joined if you'd parked in the lot instead of the street. By the time you get back to the car you find a sixty-two-year-old recovering alcoholic (a traffic warden) writing a ticket. You have a go at him, ruining his day. When he gets home after work the traffic warden takes it out on his wife. His wife has been feeling very put-upon of late, and her husband's cruel words are the final straw. She packs a bag and goes to stay with her sister two hundred miles away. In the weeks that follow, the lonely traffic warden starts drinking again. He takes booze to work and loses his job. One night at home, very drunk, he decides to

make himself dinner. The frying
pan catches fire, the fire
spreads, the house is gutted. So
is the ex-traffic warden. His
widow collects on the insurance
and passes the rest of her life
in comfort, praising his memory.

And all because you went back to
check the door.

Scenario 2. Instead of saying
good-bye to Helen in the street
where you park your car, you go
and have coffee with her. You
still get a parking ticket, but
you don't mind because you really
got on with her. Over the next
few weeks you and Helen meet
regularly. You start an affair.
Helen's husband finds out and
comes after you. He attacks you.
Defending yourself, you lash out.
He falls and cracks his head open.

You are arrested, tried, and
sentenced to four years in prison.
By the time you get out, you've
lost all ambition and confidence
and have no job. You very nearly
fall apart, but instead go to the
island of Santorini in the Aegean,
where you spend every day walking
the beach looking for coins
dropped by tourists. One day you
meet an attractive student on
vacation. She thinks you have a
cute accent and runs her fingers
through your nice thick beard and
offers to share her sleeping bag
with you. It's not until she
returns to Boston that she realizes
she's pregnant. She writes to
inform you of this, but by the
time the letter arrives you've
moved to another island, so you
never learn of the pregnancy. In
due course, she gives birth to a
boy and doesn't name him after

you. Time passes. The boy becomes a man. He meets a girl. They choose not to marry, but they bring three children into the world, the eldest of whom becomes an accountant, the second a roofing contractor, and the third an Elvis Presley impersonator. The youngest is also a serial killer who over a two-year period butchers twelve teenage girls who, between them, in time, would have given birth to twenty-nine children, who between them would have coparented sixty-eight children, who would have brought one hundred and seventy-six children into the world. This one hundred and seventy-six would have fathered or mothered four hundred and forty-two children altogether, two of whom (female twins) would have been the first living beings to

be e-mailed to Alpha Centauri,
opening the door to human
settlement in other parts of
the galaxy.
   And all because you went back to
check the door.

           Aldous U.
        Withern Rise

4.12

It was night and snowing hard as Alaric picked his
way between towering monuments and leaning
headstones. He reached the wall and bent to read the
inscription on a particular stone. It wasn't until he
saw that the name and dates were blurred and
unreadable that he understood he was dreaming.
Even so, when the ground began to shift beneath
him he grew very afraid, but the grave did not burst
open in the traditional manner. No hand reached up
and grabbed him by the ankle or throat. Yet he sensed
someone behind him and looked over his shoulder. She

was gazing at him with large, soft eyes. She uttered his name. He straightened up and held out his hands to her, but she stepped back, out of reach. He moved after her. She turned and walked away. He saw that she was limping badly. He tried to follow her, but the snow underfoot wouldn't let him. He couldn't catch her, however hard he tried, and such was his frustration that he woke. The room was awash with the surreal half dark of the snow-filled night, but he was still more in the dream than out of it, and he swung his legs over the side of the bed and sat up, thinking, I mustn't lose her again. He leaned forward, put his hands on the Folly, begged it to take him to her.

Perhaps because he was barely awake, all barriers down, it was almost instantaneous this time. The pain stormed through him, jerking him to full wakefulness even as he was propelled from the room to the garden. As the agony died, he saw where he was and felt the cold, not least from his bare feet sinking into the snow. He looked down at himself. Pajamas, outside, middle of the night. He'd read the book of this.

He glanced at the house across the lawn. It wasn't his, and he didn't want to visit it just now, but he could only return home by first reaching the Folly in Naia's room. Hardly had he thought this than a ceiling formed above him and walls clicked silently together about him. He absorbed the welcome increase in temperature. Even with the heat turned off for the night, it was warmer inside than out, here. The curtains were open. Bright shadows sprawled on the floor, rimmed the furniture. In the bed, the outline of a huddled from on her side, turned away from him, mop of dark hair peeking out from the duvet. He imagined the exquisite extra warmth in there, warm girl, legs bent at the knee, arms folded into her breasts. How tempting to slip under the cover, snuggle in to her, feel the entire length of her against him. Naia stirred, aware even in her sleep of his presence, bringing him instantly to his senses. Guilty senses. This wasn't just some girl to be lusted after, it was Naia, closer to his own flesh than any relative. He was relieved that she didn't wake, turn over, discover him standing there; but she alarmed him when she spoke—"No, Robert, get *off*!"—before once again lapsing into deep sleep. He might have wondered who Robert was, if anything more than a dream visitor, but his need to get out of there took all his attention. He turned to the bookcase, seeking the instrument that would send him home. It wasn't there.

He cast frantically about him. Where was it? What had she done with it? Had she taken it downstairs again?

Oh, there. Window ledge, other side of the bed. He leaned over the sleeper. He placed his free hand on the glass dome, pictured his own house, and with no more effort than that he was again ankle deep in snow and shivering. Now he visualized his room, and without delay a familiar unheated corner bedroom built itself around him. He was about to dive into bed and shiver the cold away when he saw something that shook him to the core.

The bed was occupied.

He stared about him. It was his room. His chair, his posters, books, clothes slung any old where, Lexie's

Folly on the bookcase. Everything exactly as it should be. So who . . . ?

He leaned over the bed. Saw the face of the sleeper. It was his own.

He jumped back. It wasn't his room. It was another just like it, in another cold, neglected Withern Rise, in which there lived another motherless Alaric Underwood. He flung himself at the Folly, gripped it with both hands, concentrated feverishly on *his* house, *his* reality. Then he was outside once more, trembling, not entirely from the cold this time. He clenched his fists, focused intently on his room, his *own* room, and . . . he was there.

Or was he? After what had happened, how could he be sure? But this bed was empty. He felt the under-sheet. Cold. Hardly conclusive proof that he hadn't come to a further variation of his reality, but it was good enough for him. He got into the chilled bed, pulled the duvet up, closed his eyes. Nothing bad could happen now. Not if he couldn't see it.

Part ③

Family Trees

Day Three

"I've phoned Mr. Dukas," Liney said when Alaric shuffled into the kitchen next morning. "He swears on his mother's life that he'll be here at twelve to fit the valve."

"Perhaps he doesn't get on with his mother."

"Yes, that occurred to me too."

"Say why he didn't come yesterday?"

"Something came up, he said. Doesn't it always? The domestics are starting at two, by the way."

"I'd forgotten the domestics."

"I thought we might go into Stone while we have a chance and look at wallpapers." Alaric's heart plummeted. "It's about time I learned how to paper," she said. "I've seen them do it on telly often enough."

"On telly they reshoot if it goes wrong."

"Ah well, do our best."

When they left the house, he was surprised to find the step clear for once. He asked where all the rubbish had gone.

"I was fed up of seeing it there," Liney told him. "I flattened the boxes by jumping on them and shoved them and the bags of papers into plastic sacks and dragged the whole lot up to the gate—four trips!—for the garbagemen to collect when next they happen by."

"Monday," he said.

They crossed the kitchen garden and opened the side gate. Out in the lane Liney set off toward the village. "This way's quicker," he said, not following. When she looked back, he jerked a thumb over his shoulder, toward the river.

"You want to *ski* there?" she said.

He started walking slowly. She came after him, legs and arms flailing wildly as if she expected to go flying at every step. He waited for her at the point where the lane turned abruptly toward Stone, circumventing Eynesford by following the river part of the way. On their left, the river reached for the distant town bridge, across which traffic moved ponderously; to their right, quite soon, the bowling green, and rising between spidery trees behind it the narrow steeple of Stone church. After ten minutes' plodding they reached the little footbridge over the boatyard. This time, this bridge, Liney did not pause and lean.

"All very pretty, I'm sure," she said as they walked over. "If viewed from behind double glazing with your back against a working radiator."

"I thought you liked being out in the snow."

"You must be thinking of someone else. I'm not built for temperatures like these." She pulled off one of her gloves with her teeth. "Dead," she said, displaying bloodless fingers.

From the bridge it was a short walk to the market square, which served as a parking lot five days a week and a marketplace on Wednesdays and Saturdays.

"Which way?" Liney asked.

"What for?"

"A shop that sells paints and wallpapers."

Alaric was as familiar with Stone as he was with Eynesford. There was no retail outlet or business in either one that he had not passed or stood outside a great many times. But put on the spot he wasn't sure that he had ever seen one that sold interior decorating materials. Liney reproached him for being so unobservant when they found just such a shop a few doors down from Underwood's Antiques & Memorabilia. The fact that her brother-in-law's shop was closed for the week did not stop Liney from peering in the window and ooohing at one or two items that took her fancy.

The hardware store, low ceilinged and rambling, boasted an impressive stock for its size. Little of this interested Alaric, but flipping indifferently through the enormous sample books while Liney poked about elsewhere, he came across the very wallpaper that he'd seen in the Long Room at Naia's. So thrilled was he to have found the paper his mother would have chosen that he offered to pay for it himself, but Liney wouldn't hear of it. She calculated the number of rolls they would need and rushed to the cashier with a credit card before his enthusiasm had a chance to give way once again to the air of sullen disinterest he affected much of the time.

Liney proved to be a better wallpaperer than she made out, though it helped that the chosen paper was self-adhesive. No need for a long, rickety trestle table, big brushes, paste slopping everywhere; just peel off the backing paper and there you were. Simple as this was, Liney, slapdash by nature, would have cheerfully hung every strip out of pattern alignment with its neighbor. This Alaric would not allow, reminding her more than once that he had to live with it.

To their surprise, Mr. Dukas arrived on the agreed dot. He had to virtually dismantle the boiler to service it and fit the valve, but he was very thorough. Afterward he went around letting air out of all fourteen of the radiators and testing them. "You really need a bigger boiler for this many rads, a house this size," he told them.

"We'll bear that in mind," Liney answered.

They were about a quarter of the way through papering the Long Room when the small army of "domestics" arrived. Alaric wasn't happy about giving a bunch of strangers unsupervised access to all parts of the house, but he could hardly follow them around. They were as efficient and conscientious as Mr. Dukas had turned out to be, and in just three hours the house was transformed. By early evening Withern Rise was cleaner than it had been for two years. Only the kitchen and the Long Room were still in disarray. The cleaners had been asked to leave these.

By seven o'clock, Alaric and Liney had finished their own task. Alaric was amazed that they had papered such a large room in a single day, and pleased with himself for not only keeping pace with Liney but correcting her tendency toward slovenliness. Working so closely with his aunt, he had discovered why nothing she attempted turned out quite as intended: the word perfection was simply not in her vocabulary. But she was a hell of a worker, he had to give her that.

3.2

Naia sat curled up on the couch in the Long Room turning the pages of a magazine while her mother drifted about straightening curtains, moving things, straightening curtains, dusting ornaments with a tissue, straightening curtains. She had been like this ever since the encounter with the boy in the cemetery yesterday. There'd been something about him. She'd wanted to reach out to him, touch him, and this, in retrospect, worried her. An attraction? Attracted to a teenage boy? God. But she thought it unlikely. It was his astounding likeness to Naia, she told herself. Yes, she'd been drawn to him by his resemblance to Naia, that was all. Damn well better be.

"Mother, you're making me nervous! Sit *down*!"

"It's these curtains. They're too long. They bunch at the bottom."

"They look fine to me. And there's nothing you can do about them anyway, so just leave them—please!"

Naia assumed that all this fiddling was just her mother being her usual self, unable to settle without something to do. She'd brought the family album up to date and would be at a loose end until she decided on her next project. Naia rarely felt guilty sitting around doing nothing. Took after her father in that respect. But for once she wished she had something to distract her. The magazine wasn't absorbing enough to keep her mind off the contents of the envelope from the message hole. Her head had been buzzing with questions ever since she read them. Questions like, who was Aldous U.? There weren't too many surnames beginning with U in the phone book, so Underwood seemed a likely candidate. But it wasn't possible. There *was* no Aldous Underwood—not a living one anyway. Of course the letter, or whatever it was, might be a hoax, intended to mystify or frustrate whoever found it. But apart from her, who else knew about the message hole? Only her parents, and Alaric perhaps. The only other person who could wander about the place at will was Mr. Knight, the occasional gardener, and he was such a serious, upright man; she couldn't see him writing things like this, sealing handmade envelopes with wax, and secreting them in trees. But if it wasn't a hoax, what was it? Some sort of philosophical treatise? A piece of imaginative fiction? Almost as puzzling as any of this was that the theme of the piece was so close to some of her own recent speculations. Was that just coincidence, or was something else at work here?

"Oh, buggeration."

Her fidgety mother had skimmed three oranges off the top of the fruit bowl with her sleeve. Naia tossed her magazine aside and jumped up.

"That's it, I'm out of here. I'm going for a walk."

Alex stooped to round up the oranges. "A walk, at this time of night? *Not* a good idea."

"It's not late."

"No, but pitch dark. Dodgy types hang around in the dark hoping ripe young specimens like you will come along."

"I'm only going around the garden."

"Oh. Well, fine then."

She was just leaving when the phone rang. "Hey, babe," Alex said into the receiver. Naia closed the door behind her and missed her father telling her mother that the trade fair was over and that even though the state of the roads had not improved, he was thinking of chancing it.

"Don't be silly, it's not worth it," Alex said to him.

"But it's so *boring*, sitting around here. This isn't exactly the Ritz, you know. And don't bother to recommend one of your lousy thrillers again. The one you lent me is about as thrilling as a vicarage tea party."

"You have a TV, don't you?"

"There's nothing on, except maybe the pay-per-view porn channels."

"So watch one of those."

"I did, last night. Made me miss the real thing. Can I come home, please?"

"No. You'll stay right where you are until the roads are safe."

"That could take *weeks*," he protested.

"We'll do our best to recognize you when you eventually return. Isn't there someone there you can talk to? What about Kate?"

"Oh, Kate was only here for one night. Cleared off before the roads got really bad. Keen to get back to the new fella."

"New fella? She didn't mention a new fella in her last letter."

"This one's just off the production line. A Tony or Tom or something. I must say, I'm crushed. I thought our Kate only had eyes for me."

"You should be so lucky."

"I seem to remember you saying something of the sort yourself at one time."

"I was just trying to boost your fragile male ego," Alex said.

3.3

He told Liney that he was going out for some air. "What, too warm for you now?" she said.

"No, it's just being cooped up indoors all day."

What this really meant was that he needed a break from her after a continuous ten or eleven hours at her side. She gave him a wonky smile as if to say that she knew this and understood. He closed the front door and stood on the step, thinking that he might call on a friend in the village. Nearest was Leonard Paine, who lived with his parents and two brothers above the little supermarket just around the corner from the school. And there was Mick Chilton a few doors down if Len wasn't in. He started toward the side gate.

It was almost nine, but the garden glowed as if lit from within, so that even without a moon or stars and with snow still falling, he had no trouble seeing his way. But he had taken no more than a couple of dozen steps when he stopped. Do I really want to see anyone? The events of the past few days were uppermost in his mind, all he could think of, but if he told his friends about such things they would think he'd cracked, word would spread, and once they were back at school he would be ridiculed mercilessly by absolutely everyone. Only one other knew about these things, and he was nervous of attempting another visit to her. The intense pain was bad enough without the knowledge that he might find himself in a reality inhabited not by Naia but by another Alaric. He imagined coming face-to-face with himself. His actual self, not a look-alike, a twin, a double, not a female version: literally another him. What would he say? What would either of them say? Or do? Could two identical minds operate in the same room? Could a person bear to look into his own eyes outside of a mirror? So many imponderables. Too many. Best to stay put. Home ground.

He turned about and headed for the river. He walked between the house and the garage, and beyond the corner that contained the River Room, left the house behind. The snow crunched agreeably under-foot as he broached the slope down to the boat land-ing. The sensible descent in such conditions was via the steps, but he felt no inclination to be sensible. He dug his heels in and half trod, half slithered down the bank. His feet struck wood, which protested but gave hardly at all. The landing was an unfussy construction of planks supported by sturdy pillars. In the non-Underwood years, an impressive motor cruiser had been moored here, but the grandest craft Alaric's family—like Naia's—had ever owned was a punt of polished mahogany that Grandpa Rayner had commissioned from the boatyard along the river. A beautiful thing, host to many a picnic on the water, the punt had been set alight and adrift one night by hooligans. It had never been replaced, but Ivan—both Ivans— had eventually bought a small rowing boat that would have been no great loss if the sabotage were repeated. They'd taken it out a few times, but it wasn't the same. Today the boat was upside down on the bank, a snow-covered air-raid shelter for dwarves.

The long platform of the boat landing was bounded to left and right by mature willows, stark and tangled now, though in summer and full leaf they reached and lolled and trailed lazily in the water. Within these bounds, this night, nothing moved or made a sound. Standing alone there, in the vast unruffled silence,

Alaric felt like the last person on earth.

"I'm the only one left."

The old man in the black coat was suddenly in Alaric's mind. The only time he'd seen this reality's version of him, he'd been loitering just across the river there. It seemed likely that in both realities he was merely some poor old boy with a wandering mind; but there'd been something in the eyes that met his in the lane at Naia's. The look of a person who'd just woken up and found that the world wasn't quite as it should be. Alaric could identify with that. Many times, even before his mother died, he'd had an unaccountable feeling that his surroundings were less real than they pretended; that the people he saw every day were somehow counterfeit, part of a performance or charade put on for his benefit. And sometimes, when walking or sitting on his own, he seemed to feel a presence or catch a movement at the utmost edge of his eye. There was never anyone there, but in the light of all that he'd learned recently it seemed reasonable to suppose, as Naia had suggested, that such sensations were glimpses into realities the thinnest of membranes away. Maybe, at such times, he almost saw or heard another version of himself: Naia perhaps. Or the other Alaric. At the instant that he thought this, the boat landing creaked. He jerked his head toward the sound, spine prickling. No one there, as ever, but the feeling came, once again, that he wasn't quite alone.

3.4

The boat landing creaked as Naia stepped down onto it. She stuck her fists in her pockets and looked at the still river, wondering what Alaric was doing just now. For all she knew he was standing on this precise spot in his reality. Being the same person in every important respect they must have done the same thing at the same moment countless times. Thought the same thought. If she seemed quicker than he, more imaginative, better informed, it was almost certainly because of the great tragedy that had befallen him. Such a terrible loss would surely dull your mind, make you very inward looking and sorry for yourself. A dulled mind was less likely to find inspiration or be intrigued by much beyond its own very limited horizons.

From Alaric, her mind drifted to family: her family; his. The missing aunt remained a mystery—why didn't she have an aunt if he did?—but she imagined that most of the other Underwoods and Bells had turned up in both realities. She'd never given much thought to family history until Alaric appeared, literally out of thin air, but often in the past few days she'd fallen to speculating about those of earlier generations who, simply by existing, had conspired to bring her into the world and to this point in time. They, too, had been young once. Probably not so very different from people living today in ways that mattered. She wondered if she had the looks, attitudes, mannerisms of any of her forebears; similar skills, tastes, ambitions. Perhaps, if one of them found a way to step forward in time and join her here, they might be like sisters, with everything in common. Maybe one or two earlier Underwoods had come out here on a night just like this and also reflected on those who'd stood here before them. They were gone now, all of them, as she would be gone someday, but there was an odd comfort in the thought that she was merely the latest of her line to stand on this spot, musing on her part in things. Her position. Her role.

3.5

From the landing Alaric rambled about the grounds, making casual patterns in the snow with his feet. He was in the south garden when an unexpected wind sprang up, a very sharp wind that chilled him to the bone. He scurried for cover behind the Family Tree, from where he watched the wind ripple the snow's powdery surface, listened to it whistling through the umbrella of boughs and branches overhead. When he felt a quivering sensation where his shoulder touched the tree, he placed the flat of his hands on the trunk, sure that he was imagining it. But the tree was indeed quivering. Was such a thing possible? Could a wind, even one this spirited, buffet an oak of such girth? He was still wondering this when a terrible sorrow swept through him, a sorrow so incalculable that it consumed him utterly, driving him to his knees. So stricken was he with grief for a tragedy he knew nothing of that he barely noticed the tree jump beneath his hands; but then he fell away from it, and the great sorrow ceased at once. He leaped up and walked toward the house, suddenly very eager to be inside.

Reaching the front door, he turned the handle. It felt strange, less firm than it should, but what concerned him more was that the door was locked. Liney. He'd only been gone a few minutes and the batty old twit had locked him out. She'd turned off the hall light too, the light he'd made a point of leaving on to illuminate the step through the window for his return. He was further surprised to see that the window was open, but at least he had a way in without summoning her. With any luck he'd be able to sneak up to his room and snaffle an extra half hour's peace before slipping back down and pretending to have just returned. It wasn't easy to climb in, the

window being so small, but he managed it. The ledge
had a spongy feel, which he couldn't explain and didn't
have time to think about before he was inside and it
ceased to matter. The window was an old sash,
impossible to close silently, so he left it open, intending to shut it later. There was just enough snow light
for him to see by. He sat on the mat and whipped off
his boots. He could hear the TV in the Long Room
to his left. Liney must have decided to leave the
clearing up until tomorrow. Fine by him. He headed
for the stairs. There were no lights on in the lower
hall, but there was one on upstairs, sufficient for him
to notice various idiosyncrasies that, in fact, he
missed, because creeping through the house like a
spy took all his concentration.

He started up, intent on making as little noise as
possible, and again failed to notice differences that
would ordinarily have leaped out at him. When he
reached the halfway platform, he saw a light around
the bathroom door. She wasn't downstairs then. He
was estimating the odds of making it past the bath-

room without being heard when a loud voice reached him from the main bedroom.

"Wally, where the fuck are you?"

His legs almost gave way under him. Dad's voice. But how . . . ?

"I'm 'aving a slash, d'ya mind?" This from the bathroom.

"The rest of 'em could be back any time," the first voice shouted. "Get a move on!"

Not his father's voice. Similar, but coarser, harder. Alaric pressed himself into the long shadow that fell like a cloak from the landing to the turn of the stairs; just in time, for a small man in a black leather jacket left the bathroom zipping his fly. Who were these men? What were they doing here? And where was Liney? Mystified, fighting alarm, he at last noticed the pictures, the wallpaper, the fussy stair carpet, painted banister rail.

"It's mostly shit," the voice reminiscent of his dad's said in the master bedroom. "Hardly worth the bother."

"You said they was loaded," said the other, joining him.

"They are. Have to be. Have you seen their fucking car?"

"There might be a safe somewhere. . . . "

"Yeah. Go take a look."

"Where?"

"How would I know? Anywhere, everywhere, use your head."

"I'm not goin' back in that bloody room."

"Why? Think they'll leap up and wrestle you to the ground, do you?"

"You didn't have to do that, Ive."

"Yes, I did. They saw our faces. Now stop whining and move it."

The man in the leather jacket went into the room occupied by Liney at home. At home. This wasn't his Withern. Or Naia's. So whose? Whoever it belonged to, these men were turning it over while they were out. That made them dangerous. Alaric backed down the stairs, avoiding the creakers.

3.6

Naia could have climbed the steps up from the landing, but the temptation to clamber over the bank was hard to resist. She lost her footing before she made it to the top, however, and came down on her hands and knees. Then her legs slid out from under her, and for a moment she feared she would slither backward, hit the landing, and somersault dramatically into the river—or onto it, if the ice was as thick as she imagined. She made hooks of her hands and dug in above her head. When her grip held, she gave a hearty "Hoo!" and pulled herself up. Reaching the flatter ground above, she laughed to show invisible observers what fun that had been and walked on to the house, brushing snow off her.

She passed between the pair of grim black yews—disapproving sentries—and sat for a minute on one of the benches in the porch, wondering what to do next. When nothing came to her, she decided to go back in. Her mother would say, "Was it worth it?," because she hadn't been gone very long at all, and she would say,

"Cold out," and Mum would say, "I could have told you that," and they would stoke the fire and put in a couple of hours in front of the box, and that would be the day gone.

The porch door being locked, she had to go all the way around, and when she got in, Alex gave her the gist of her telephone conversation with Ivan. Naia was pleased to hear about Kate and the boyfriend. Nothing could excuse her father for what he would have done if Mum hadn't been there to keep him and the house in order, but she was glad to be able to set aside the suspicious notions that had begun to fester about him and Kate alone together in Bristol.

3.7

From the bottom of the stairs Alaric slipped into the Long Room and stood behind the door trying to hold himself together. The TV blared from the far end. Some rowdy game show. Bewildered and frightened, he barely registered that there was no reason for the television to be on if the only people in the house were burglars. The subdued lighting was provided by tulip-shaped wall lights that would never have found their way into a house of which an Alex Underwood had charge. She wouldn't have chosen the flocked wallpaper either, or displayed the job lot of studio portraits of freckled kids with unfortunate smiles and missing teeth. The only furniture at this end of the room was a modern teak writing bureau, a matching sideboard, and a 1950s walnut display cabinet with fancy scroll-work on the glass doors. The cabinet contained a collection of decorative plates and nauseatingly pretty figurines of Italian abstraction.

Alaric shook himself. I have to get out of here. Rather than go back the way he'd come and risk being seen from the landing, he set off along the room toward the door that would return him to the upper hall and the window by which he'd entered. As at home, and at Naia's, armchairs and a big couch took up most of the TV end of the room, though the ones here were excessively floral. Briefly puzzling over a wedge-shaped log on the floor, he saw over the back of the couch that the original fireplace no longer existed here, its place taken, in small part, by a flame-effect gas fire. Beside the fire stood a shiny black log basket with ornate brass curlicues. The logs in the basket had no practical function. As he approached, something else caught his eye just below the top of the couch. Stretching up, he saw the dome of a bald head with wisps of white hair.

There was someone there. Someone who had only to glance over his shoulder to see him.

Alaric moved silently toward the door. He was almost there when it occurred to him that the burglars were banging about so loudly upstairs that even a game-show fan couldn't fail to hear them. Yet the man on the couch didn't move a muscle. Was he deaf? If so, he couldn't be enjoying the show much: no subtitles. Reaching the door, he looked along the couch. There were two people on it, not one. An elderly couple. The man sat upright, and his wife lay half across him. She seemed to be asleep, while the man's head lolled a little. The one eye that Alaric could see in profile stared in the direction of the TV. Unblinking. Something wrong here. At the risk of being caught, he craned his neck until he could see part of the far side of the man's head.

There was a massive dent in the old man's skull, and the right eye looked as if it had burst. His shirt and the couch on that side of him were stained with blood. Suddenly the log on the carpet made sense. The woman might have been treated similarly, or she might not, but as she was facedown he couldn't see any evidence to prove it. Perhaps her heart had given out when the men rushed in and one of them seized the log from the basket and struck her husband his death blow.

Crashes from upstairs. Raised male voices.

Turning to the door, Alaric misjudged its position and bumped into a little telephone table. It was an odd sort of bumping, like nudging marshmallow. He looked at the phone. He ought to call the police. Isn't that what you do in situations like this? There might be time to call before he made a break for it. His hand closed around the receiver and lifted it. It slipped through his fingers. He picked it up again, and again failed to hold it. This time it fell on its side on the table. Puzzled, he leaned over the phone and listened for a dial tone. It was there. If he couldn't get a grip on the thing, he could surely manage to press one little button three times. He touched the nine. The button went down, but not far enough. He stabbed at it. The button resisted. No matter how hard he pressed, it would go no farther than halfway. The dial tone continued without pause. It was like the meeting with Naia in the garden yesterday, before he was absorbed into her reality. Nothing, including her, had real substance for him. So. Somehow, within the past ten or fifteen minutes, he had strayed into this reality, but instead of waiting to be drawn into the house from the garden, if it was possible here, he had crawled through the window and—

Thud, thud, thud. Heavy feet on the stairs.

He leaped at the door and yanked the handle, intending to run into the hall, grab his boots, and jump out the window before he could be seen. The door opened, but only a little. He tugged again. Another few inches and that was it. He turned sideways, tried to squeeze through. The gap was insufficient, but the door itself proved no obstacle. One half of him passed through the wood. He felt it, but only as a mild discomfort. On the other side, he pressed back into the recessed doorway and looked along the hall; saw the man in the leather jacket cross from the stairs to the River Room. His entry was followed by crashes as he set about tearing the room apart in his search for a safe or valuables.

Alaric snatched up the boots he'd left on the mat and chucked them through the window. Climbing after them he sat on the step to pull them on, trying to decide where to go from there. His own footprints, surprisingly shallow given the depth of the snow, pointed the way in reverse. He got up and ran across the garden, dreading a yell as someone came after him wielding a weapon. There was no yell, no pursuit, but he reached the tree just moments before the fractured beam of headlights appeared in the twiggy tunnel along the drive; then a white Mercedes was drawing up in front of the house and three kids were tumbling out. Their parents stepped out at a more leisurely pace. The man, who'd been driving, said to his wife: "Put the kettle on while I put her away, Sal, I'm gasping."

"What did your last slave die of?" she replied.

"Love," the man said, clumping toward the garage.

The children were already stamping their feet on the step. "Mum! Hurry *up*! Cold!" Their mother inserted a key in the lock, and they pushed past her. The light came on. As her husband pulled the garage doors back, she followed the kids in.

While Alaric watched all this from behind the Family Tree, the two intruders, making a hasty exit from a ground-floor window on the river side of the house, ran for cover far to his left. The man in the leather jacket was a petty thief and occasional burglar called Wally Musgrave, who as a boy had exchanged his grand-mother's false teeth for a model racing car. The taller man, organizer of the break-in, had prior convictions for aggravated assault and robbery with violence. Twice divorced, he had two children from his first marriage, Adam and Nicole, but his violent history had led to a court order forbidding him to see them. His name was Ivan Charles Underwood. His family had once owned Withern Rise, way back, long before his time, and all his life he'd resented the people who lived there instead of him. What was so special about them that they could have so much while he had to scratch around for a living? Well, he thought with amusement, the place would never be the same for them after this. The dead or the living.

Alaric did not witness the men's escape, but he heard the screams inside the house and saw the driver of the Mercedes running for the door. He'd just reached it when Alaric felt a tremor from the tree he was hiding behind and the screams ended, like a tape arbitrarily spliced. He blinked. The Mercedes was gone. The garage doors were closed. There was a light in an upper window, with Liney moving across it.

He pushed himself away from the tree and made for the house. This time the window would be shut, the door unlocked.

3.8

Naia and her mother had been chatting with the TV turned down, laughing about something stupid Dad once did. Naia had excused herself to go to the bathroom. She went upstairs, but not to the bathroom. She had to keep looking in her room in case Alaric made an impromptu visit. She wasn't sure what he would do if he came and she wasn't there. Come looking for her perhaps, the prospect of which made her very nervous. She went into her room. Alaric wasn't there. But someone was.

"Mum?"

There was only one route upstairs, and Naia had just taken it. There was no way her mother could have gotten there before her. But here she was, sitting on the bed, sobbing into her hands.

"Mum, what are you . . . ? How? I don't . . . "

Her mother neither replied nor looked up. Naia's bewilderment increased further when she heard a name between the sobs.

"Alaric. Oh, Alaric. My love."

Her mother, who simply could not be there, had no idea that Alaric existed, yet here she was wailing his name as if he'd just died or someth—

The Alex Underwood on the bed had vanished, taking her sorrow with her. There wasn't even a dent where she'd been sitting.

3.9

Alaric closed the front door, locked it, put his back against it. The shock was beginning to catch up with him. He stayed where he was, leaning against the door, listening intently. All quiet. No sound of the TV this time.

"Alaric? That you?"

Liney, coming toward him from the stairs. She smiled when she saw him, but drawing near, getting a better look at him, the smile faded.

"Are you all right?"

"Yeah, fine."

He turned away to remove his coat and ease his boots off. Liney hovered. Teenage boys weren't a species she'd ever had much to do with, even when a teenager herself. Conversation with them had always been like trying to communicate in a dead language.

"I've cleared just enough space to sit down in there," she said, indicating the Long Room. "One or two of your videos I wouldn't mind seeing. *Donnie Darko* or *Final Destination*. What do you say?"

Alaric recalled all too vividly the old couple on the couch in the other Long Room. Different couch, but the same position. He couldn't sit in that space, even here. Not tonight.

"Tired," he said.

Halfway upstairs he heard again the conversation between the two men on that other landing. His skin crawled; stomach turned. He rushed up to the bathroom, flung up the toilet seat, and vomited so stridently that Liney couldn't miss it, even downstairs. She came running and was leaning over him before he'd finished, patting his back, making soothing noises that soothed not at all.

She helped him up, flushed the bowl, put down the

seat while he slushed cold water in his face and rinsed his mouth out.

"What brought that on?"

His reply was little more than a grunt. She guided him to his room, but he couldn't face lying down immediately. Liney draped his duvet around him. He tugged it across his chest. He was shaking.

"Anything I can get you?" she asked. "Cup of tea? Glass of water?"

"Water," he said, to get rid of her for a minute as much as anything. She left the room, pleased to be of use.

Without her there to distract him, the corpse or corpses on the other couch again filled his mind. Who were those people? Not Underwoods, obviously. Sick as he felt, he concocted a possibility. In 1963 Grandpa Rayner had bought Withern back from the family who'd owned it since the late forties. Maybe the deal had had an equal chance of success or failure, and a reality had come into being in which Rayner hadn't been able to raise enough money, or his offer had been rejected, so that the Underwoods of that reality had never moved back. A son, and his wife, of the resident family—or a daughter and her husband—had also lived there, and when they too became parents they were given a part of the house for their own use. The arrangement had worked well enough until tonight, when the lives of the two who'd kept the place going all these years were terminated horribly by a pair of evil bastards looking for trinkets. He saw how it might be for the survivors. The middle-aged parents would become terrified of shadows and sounds in the night, and their kids, wherever they went in the world, would be haunted all their lives by the sight that had met their eyes when they burst into the Long Room that terrible February evening of 2005, when they were young.

3.10

She couldn't account for it. Her mother downstairs in the Long Room and up in her bedroom at one and the same time, the one upstairs sobbing a name she couldn't possibly know and disappearing before her eyes. Could she have been the ghost of Alaric's mother? Were ghosts able to wander in dimensions other than the ones they'd inhabited when alive? That might explain the sobbing. Mourning the loss of a beloved son. It was she who had died, but the loss would have been as great for her as for him, in a way. The only trouble was that Naia didn't believe in ghosts. Ghosts were hogwash. But if the Alex in her room was not a ghost but a living person, where had she come from? Where did she belong? And why had she been sobbing her heart out over Alaric?

3.11

Liney returned with a glass of water. A giant glass. She never does things by halves, he thought.

"How are you feeling?"

She held the glass to his lips, which made it impossible to answer without creating a wet aunt, so again he merely grunted. She sat down beside him and put her arms around him, began rocking him like a baby.

Rocking was not something he really wanted to do just then, but it seemed churlish to pull away, so they sat like this for some time, rocking silently back and forth, until their mutual self-consciousness became tangible.

"Better now?" Liney asked.

"Mm."

She set him free. "Want to lie down?"

" 'Kay."

He stretched out and she arranged the duvet over him. Neither of them mentioned the fact that he was still fully dressed. She went to the door and turned off the light.

"I'll pop in later to see how you are."

" 'Kay."

As she went downstairs Liney's imagination kicked in. He'd been to a mate's in the village and drunk something that didn't agree with him, or smoked some bad dope. Had to be something like that. A teenage boy doesn't go out on a freezing winter night in reasonable spirits and health and return deathly pale half an hour later, puking and shivering, if he's just been strolling in the garden. She was unsure whether to phone his father or carry on as though nothing had happened. If she told Ivan about this she ran the risk of alienating Alaric just as they were beginning to feel at ease with each other. But if she kept her suspicions to herself . . .

While Liney was reviewing her choices, Alaric, swaddled in feather and down, closed his eyes and stumbled into sleep. Fortunately, next morning, he did not recall his dreams.

_____Day Two

2.1

Since last night Alaric's nervousness about attempting further visits to Naia's had increased considerably. He might find himself back at the Murder House (as he was already calling it). What would it be like there today? Buzzing with police and forensics, no doubt. A cordon around the property. TV crews, reporters, and neighbors peering over the walls and trying to get up the drive, testing the ice for a glimpse or picture from the river.

To take his mind off these things, he tried to concentrate on the most mundane aspects of life at his own version of the house, which meant helping Liney clear up the mess they'd made while the domestics were doing their stuff elsewhere. The kitchen was the worst, with paint pots, brushes, and solvents everywhere. The stove was beyond reach, so Liney rang out for fried chicken.

"I feel terrible, not providing better fare for you," she said.

"So you should," he said, tucking in with a will.

It was while they were eating that she threw him a bit of a curve.

"How do you feel about Kate and your dad now? Warming to the idea, or . . . "

"She's after his money," he said, brusquely.

"Money?"

"The settlement."

"Oh, the settlement, I'd forgotten that."

"Bet she hasn't. It'll be at least two hundred grand, you know."

"A tidy sum," Liney said. "Wouldn't mind it myself. But I doubt that it's enough for a woman of any intelligence to pick up and throw in her lot with a slob like your father. Have to be pretty desperate for that."

"Maybe she is."

"Did she strike you as a gold digger when you met her?"

"She's very clever," he said gruffly.

But these were just words, conjured out of the moment. The truth was that his feelings about Kate were no longer as clear-cut as they had been. A few days ago he'd hated her, pure and simple. She was an outsider about to impose herself on his life. No matter that his life was a grim trudge, devoid of light and hope; Kate Faraday had no place in it. But that was before Naia, before the other Withern Rise and the chance encounter in the cemetery. Today he was no longer sure what he felt about Kate. He almost preferred it the other way. You knew where you were when you hated someone.

In the afternoon, needing other things to think about, he called on Len and Mick in the village. They were both out. He went on to Stone, looked in shop windows, quickly became bored, and ambled home again via the boatyard bridge. He didn't go indoors immediately, however, but to the south garden, the Family Tree. He'd been putting this off but could do so no longer. He'd climbed this tree all through childhood, scrambled along its boughs and branches to his heart's content, monkeyed about in it on his own or with friends until the age of thirteen or fourteen. Growing up, it had seemed the best tree in all the world. But after last night he was suspicious of it. And nervous. He hadn't previously given a thought as to why the tree was the stopping-off point between the realities, but he'd woken this morning with an idea that had grown in him through the day and was with him still: that it was the tree, not the Follies, that linked the realities.

He tried to reason it out, as Naia would have done, starting with the supposition, implausible even to him, that when the limbs of a tree fall or are removed the connection between the separated parts remains.

The model houses in the glass shades, carved of wood from variations of the tree, were consequently linked to it—and to one another. The physical link, and the resultant interchange, might or might not have been sparked by Naia's "factors." There'd been no wooden replica to draw him into the non-Underwood Withern Rise, he was sure of that. But there had been something.

The logs. They, too, must have been formerly attached to a Family Tree, perhaps as part of the bough that had come down one night in a high wind. When one of the logs was used to bludgeon the old man to death, the tree it had belonged to absorbed the misery inflicted by its former component and passed it on to versions of itself in neighboring realities. Alaric, sheltering behind one of them, had received the emotion, full force. The slight jolt, or lurch, that he'd hardly noticed while trying to cope with the overwhelming sorrow, was his tree transferral him to the reality in which the anguish was initiated. He guessed that it was an involuntary transferral, something the tree couldn't help or control. It had stood in the garden for a full century, growing and maturing over the body of Withern's creator. During those ten decades, the tree had been exposed to the emotions of those who climbed it, leaned against it, lived their lives around it. By being there at the heart of things, heart of the garden, the Family Tree had become vulnerable to the variety and scope of human feeling; developed a capacity to shuttle emotionally affected Underwoods—two of them anyway—between the realities in which it stood. As for why he'd felt no pain when transferred from tree to tree, could it be that starting from the tree itself was simply more direct?

It was crazy, of course. Pure balls. A tree with feelings? Ludicrous. The stuff of fantasy. And yet . . . it fitted. But whether he'd gotten it right or wildly wrong, he knew he had to tell Naia. Being so annoyingly bright, she might see a whole bunch of flaws in his reasoning, but nevertheless he felt a duty to warn her. If he was even half right about the tree, she might lean against it at some point and be transported to a

Withern Rise she would never willingly visit. One plagued by Naia-hungry wolves perhaps. Now there was a thought.

2.2

Friends had again called and texted during the day to ask Naia if she wanted to go somewhere or do something, but she'd continued to decline. Tied to the house in case Alaric appeared, the highlight of the day was the delivery of the new dining suite for the River Room. Early evening now, and she and her mother were having tea on trays and watching a DVD rented from the newsagent's. When the phone rang and her mother said, "That'll be your dad," she said, "Well tell him to ring back." She might have forgiven him for having an affair in another reality, but how dare he interrupt a film she'd been looking forward to?

Ivan had phoned to say that he'd decided to risk the journey in spite of the dodgy roads. Alex argued, but he was adamant. He was coming home tomorrow, and that was final.

"It's very inconvenient," she said. "I'll have to kick the lover out."

"We all have to make sacrifices," he replied.

Later, Naia sat on her bed looking through the more recent pages of the updated family album. Her entire life was documented in this book. Alaric's mother would have put together a similar album, she realized. More than similar; identical in every way, except . . .

She sat bolt upright. Why hadn't she thought of it before?

She moved up the bed until she was sitting on her pillows and started going through the album again, from the beginning. There was a photo of her aged two and a half, in a blue summer dress. Her hair was fairer then, piled up on top of her head and bursting out of a purple scrunchie like a fountain. If there was a picture of Alaric on the same page in his album, what would he be wearing? Probably not a summer dress and a scrunchie. She turned more pages, passing slowly through the years and photo after photo of her at various ages and phases. Where there were pictures of her with friends, she imagined pictures in Alaric's album of him with different friends. What friends? Did she know them in her reality? Did she like them?

And then there were the holiday snaps. Had he and his parents gone on the same holidays as she and hers, at the same time? Had they done the same things, exactly the same way? Taken the same pictures, only with him in them instead of her? She came to a photo taken five or six years ago on a Pembrokeshire beach. It showed her and Mum holding ice-cream cones. Just before Dad clicked the shutter, they dipped their noses in the ice cream. Was there a picture in Alaric's book of him and his mother with ice cream on *their* noses?

And what about that aunt of his? The aunt she didn't have. He hadn't wanted to talk about her, but he'd said her name. Something like Lena, or Limey. Limey? Nickname maybe. Perhaps she'd traveled in America. She might be in some of the pictures in Alaric's album. Where? Which pages? And what pictures would be on those pages in *her* album?

Finally there were the photos from the past two

years. Had Alaric and his dad continued to take pictures when there were just the two of them? Unlikely, but even if they had, had they stuck them in the album? She doubted this, too. People who let their house go as badly as they had wouldn't give much priority to the upkeep of a family album.

It was the necessary differences between the two albums that determined her to give Alaric till ten in the morning to come to her. Dad would be home sometime in the afternoon, so it had to be the morning. If Alaric hadn't showed by ten she would go to him, taking her album with her. He might not want to look at it, but that was his problem. She would insist on comparing it with his. It might even be worth the risk of bumping into the nameless aunt.

_____ Day One

1.1

His father had phoned late last night to say that he and Kate were coming home today, snow or no snow. This had had a galvanizing effect on Liney. She was up at first light and crashing about downstairs, inflicting her misguided concept of order on the house. When Alaric went down and found her in the utility room with a huge basket of clothes, he decided that this would be a good time to make himself scarce.

"Gotta go out," he said.

"You haven't had breakfast," she replied, shoving laundry into the machine.

"I'll grab a cereal bar."

"Well before you go fetch all your dirty wash down, would you? That pile of stuff in your dad's wardrobe too. I don't see how I'll ever get everything done before they get here. It's my own fault, allowing myself to sleep last night. And after the washing there's the ironing, and then there's the—"

"You don't have to do these things," he said impatiently. "It's not your job."

"Of course it's not my job," she answered. "But put yourself in Kate's position. How would you like it if you arrived at your new home and had to become the family skivvy five minutes after getting your coat off?"

Alaric went upstairs, gathered all the grubby clothes he could find, and carried them down to the washing machine sideways, nose averted from his load, parts of which smelled none too sweet.

"Doesn't your father know how to use this?" Liney asked when she saw the size of the bundle. "Or you, come to that?"

"We manage."

"Not too well by the look of it. Clothes don't wash themselves, you know."

"I have to go," he said.

"It's all right for some."

"Going out the back way."

"Why the back way?"

"Look at the river."

He wasn't going out the back way, but he couldn't risk not being seen leaving by the front door. He put on his parka and boots and walked rather too loudly down the hall to the door in the back porch, which he unlocked and unbolted, again very loudly, before running silently upstairs. He was in his room, reaching for the Folly, when he remembered the album. He'd brought it up last night to take with him today, wanting to compare it with Naia's. She would be bound to have a family album too; a more complete one. He picked up the shopping bag and laid his free hand on the dome of the Folly, hoping fervently that if it worked at all it would send him to her reality, not one of those others.

1.2

Ten fifteen and still he hadn't come. Well, he'd had his chance. Shopping bag in hand, Naia faced the Folly, which for ease of use she'd returned to the bookcase. She placed the palm of her free hand on the dome and did her best to really want to see Alaric. She would have been more wholehearted in this if she'd not been dreading the coming agony. Her palm tingled, and she prepared herself as well as she could; but then, to her surprise, the room dissolved and she was outside, under the tree, before she'd fully registered the pain. There was little time to be pleased by the speed of the transition, however, for at once a room began to grow about her.

Her own room.

Concluding that she must have done something wrong or not tried hard enough, she closed her eyes and focused on Alaric, Alaric's room, Alaric's Withern Rise. The tingling again, then the pain leaping briefly up her arm, her feet plunging into snow, the cold enfolding her. She opened her eyes. The great tree, fanning out hugely above her, was translucent, and somewhere in it a room, her room, was again forming. Then she was back once more, standing by the bookcase and the Folly.

Her frustration, though considerable, was short-lived. Before she could make a third attempt a tug-of-war commenced between the tree and her room. One moment she was in the garden, the next indoors, then outside, then in her room, dizzy, reeling, increasingly frightened, unable to stop it, take stock, catch breath. Then, suddenly, she was careering toward the tree. She threw her arms over her face, expecting the worst, but just short of the tree a figure whooshed out of thin air, crashed into her, and the two of them were jostling for position and place.

It had been the same for Alaric, dragged helplessly from room to garden, garden to room, hurtling finally toward the tree, where someone—Naia—rushed at him and was at once fighting him for a space they both must occupy. They thrashed about like trapped animals, fighting to keep separate, hold on to their identities, while their twin realities fought to meld them into one in pursuit of easy logic.

"No! No! We're not—"

"The house! Think—"

"We're not the same!"

"—house. Inside the house!"

Walls and ceiling filling in. Two rooms, imprecisely superimposed, two people close to becoming one. Resisting.

"Pull apart! Pull . . . *apart*!"

The garden drew them but held them for moments only, quivering, before the room reclaimed them. Garden again now, and room again, garden, room, flung this way, that, struggling, but fusing into one body, one life, one hist—

"No! We're two! Concentrate! We're *different*!"

Pause. Time stops.

Then, slowly, the rooms divide by the tiniest degree.

"I think it's working."

"Yes."

"Oh—wait!"

In the fleeting halfway garden they reach for bags dropped in the struggle.

"Okay! Now! *Separate*!"

Furnishings, books, pictures, favored relics of childhood.

Apart. Alone.

A small cracking sound like the shell of an egg. Glass dome imploding. The carved house folds in upon itself. In separate rooms two shades, two perfect houses, shatter beyond hope of repair.

1.3

Naia was too numb to move. She had fallen into her chair, and when her mother knocked she continued to sit there, staring at the small heap of splintered glass and wood. The circular base, cut from another tree long ago, was all that remained.

"Oh, you are here. Why didn't you answer? Listen, you know the . . . " The sentence was never finished. A gasp. "That isn't the Folly. Oh, what happened?"

Still she could find no answer. All she could think

was that never again would she be able to receive Alaric, or visit him, and so much still to work out. It wasn't just the loss of knowledge, though. With time she would have worn down that deep-seated belligerence of his, and when the real Alaric emerged from his cocoon of despair, they would have become as close as the closest brother and sister. How could they not, knowing all that they did, firsthand, of each other's lives?

"Oh, Naia, I should never have let you have it up here."

She could see how it looked. But what could she say? What credible defense could she offer? The model house, the best thing her mother had ever made, looked as if a miniature wrecking ball had been repeatedly swung against it from all sides, until there was nothing left of it. Alex's dismay flared into anger. She whirled around.

"Well? Nothing to say for yourself?"

Naia shrank from her. Mum didn't often lose it, but when she did, she was far more formidable than Dad in one of his impotent sputtering rages.

"And what are you doing up here with your boots on? Boots with *snow* on them? In your *room*? Naia, what is this? What are you *playing* at?"

She hadn't had a chance to remove her boots or her coat. She hadn't even put the shopping bag down, just collapsed into the chair, shocked, defeated, exhausted.

"Honest to God, girl, it's about time you started behaving responsibly! I sometimes think you haven't the sense you were born with. I am so . . . so *disappointed* in you!"

With which Alex Underwood rushed out, in tears of loss that even she couldn't explain.

1.4

Alaric couldn't have said why he took the family album out of the shopping bag and started to turn the pages. It might have been the need to distract himself, take his mind off the suddenly unreachable, the magnitude of his loss.

Whatever the reason, the differences, when he began to notice them, were so marked they took his breath away. The bib was one of the first. What should have been a blue bib covered in baby elephants was a pink one with cute little rabbits all over it. Then there were the photos of him cuddling dolls, with bows in his hair. It wasn't until he reached a picture of a gleeful one-year-old standing up in a bubble bath (what a shock *that* was!) that it all became clear. He wondered if Naia had yet noticed that they'd picked up the wrong bags in the garden. She was going to have a real problem explaining his album. He would just put this one away somewhere and deny all knowledge if his father asked after it. No big worry there anyway. Dad never looked at the album. He had no wish to be reminded of the past. But Alex Underwoods weren't like that. They liked to know where everything was at all times. Just for once he was glad he wasn't in Naia's shoes.

Almost every photograph in her book had had a faithful counterpart in his. The only person missing was Liney. There weren't a great many of her in his album, but there were none at all here, as of course there couldn't be. Other pictures had been substituted, mostly snaps discarded by his mother when putting her album together. The pictures of Naia were the most interesting. Wherever he appeared in his album, she appeared in this one, in the same settings, doing the same things, at the same frozen instant. In most of the early shots, wearing unisex dungarees, similar pajamas and so on, they could have been the same child; but as the years moved along she appeared in dresses and skirts and little-girl sandals and took to wearing plastic jewelry, and her hair was allowed to reach her shoulders or was shown plaited or in bunches. But even here her expressions deviated very little from his, in his corresponding pictures.

It wasn't only the photos, though. There was a dent in the thick green cover of this album, where, like his own, it had once been dropped. And there was a small brown stain—spilled coffee—on a photo of Naia and her dad trying to look terrified beside a life-size dinosaur at Blackgang Chine: a perfect match for the stain on the same picture in his book, in which *he* stood making faces with *his* dad.

It was with trembling fingers that he approached the cutoff point: the first of the many pages that were empty in his book. He turned the page. No pictures had been taken for two or three months after the accident, but then they started, with a vengeance, as if Ivan, suddenly the family's main photographer, had at last gotten it together and didn't intend to let a single event or visit or situation go unrecorded. There were so many pictures of Alex, at first quite frail and underweight, leaning on a walking stick, gradually recovering from her ordeal, gaining strength and color as spring gave way to summer and they started to get out more. He recognized the settings for a few of the photos, but there were many that meant nothing to him. If his mother had lived, his album—now in Naia's possession—would have contained pictures like these; identical in every respect, except that he would be in them, not her.

1.5

The last snow had fallen by lunchtime. By early afternoon the sun was nosing through the clouds. With her father due back anytime, Naia slipped out the side gate and turned right. She climbed the cemetery steps. At the top she scanned the whitened graveyard. No Alex Underwood was buried here, of course, but now that all access to Alaric's world was denied, she wanted to try and identify the spot where they had put her in their version of the cemetery. They would have chosen a place of some relevance or significance, she thought, though she couldn't imagine what or where it could be. The sun cast her shadow before her, elongated and blue, as she drifted this way and that between the memorials, seeking inspiration, willing to settle for intuition. None came, but after a while she happened near the ivy-laden wall that separated the cemetery from the house. Here her gaze fell upon a headstone she'd never noticed before. It had always been there, but she'd never been one for dallying in graveyards. The stone leaned against the wall, almost wearily, within an arc of ivy. She read the legend chiseled into it.

ALDOUS UNDERWOOD

BELOVED SON AND BROTHER

1934–1945

She frowned. *Another* Aldous? Suddenly the world was full of them. First the bishop under the Family Tree, then the writer of the mysterious letter, now an eleven-year-old of that name. The boy had died in the last year of the Second World War. As a casualty of the war, she wondered, or of some unrelated illness or accident? Being an Underwood, in this cemetery, he must have been a relative; most likely living at Withern. By her estimate he had died nineteen years before her father was born; not so long ago really, and yet . . . she'd never heard of him.

Ah, well.

She turned away, still with no more idea where they might have buried Alaric's mother than what to do about the family album she'd brought home by mistake. An album stuffed with pictures of a boy instead of her, with two years' worth of missing pages—pages her mother had only just completed.

1.6

He sat on the floor of his room, staring at the black window, devoid for once of tumbling snowflakes. Down in the kitchen, Liney's singing was at its demented worst as she prepared a "special" meal. He dreaded to think what "special" meant. He didn't really care anyway. It was over. That was all he knew. He'd seen all he was going to of the other Withern Rise, of the way things might have been for him; could have been. Of course, there was still the tree. No telling what the tree could do, where it could take him if . . .

No. It was over. Time to face reality. His own reality. And the truth of things: that his mother wasn't coming back, that Kate was coming instead, that things would be different. It might not be so bad. His mother had liked Kate. That is, Naia's mother had, and that was good enough for him. Had to be. It was all there was.

The clang of the old doorbell loped through the house, collecting echoes. The signal to move on. He got up and went out to the stair landing; he stood looking down. He couldn't see right along the hall from there, but he heard Liney open the front door, shout a greeting, his father's gruff response: "I don't know, locked out of my own house."

"Safety precaution," Liney said. "How were the roads?"

"Roads? Don't talk to me about roads. You wouldn't know sanding had been invented. Here we are, twenty-first century, and—"

"Shut up, you miserable git, and introduce us."

"Hmm! Liney, this is Kate. Kate, this is the mad old bat I've been telling you about."

"Kate!"

Alaric imagined Liney reaching for her and hugging the breath out of her, then pulling her inside. He heard the door close, feet stomping on the mat, and Dad asking what was burning and where all the heat was coming from. Liney answered both questions. He sounded quite pleased about the second.

"Turn my back for one minute, and . . ." He'd noticed the Long Room through the open door to his left. "Stone me."

"You gave us permission, remember? Don't you like it?"

"Tell you when I get over the shock."

"I'm not taking all the blame," Liney said. "That son of yours. What a slave driver. And talk about perfectionist."

"Where is he anyway?"

His father stepped into the hall, Kate and Liney trailing after him, already chatting intimately. The Kate Faraday Alaric looked down upon from the landing was a Kate he'd virtually forgotten—cheerful, enthusiastic, warm—not the cold, calculating bitch he'd turned her into in his mind. She saw him before anyone else did.

"Alaric!" she cried, as though spotting a long-lost relative.

He couldn't find his voice immediately but managed a small wave as he walked to the head of the stairs. Well, here goes, he thought, and swallowed hard. There was a peculiar tightness in his chest as he started down.

_____Turnback:
Alternative

. . . thrashing about like trapped animals, fighting to retain their—

"No! No! We're not the same!"

"The house! Think house. Inside the house!"

Walls and ceiling filling in. Two rooms, two people, merging into one.

"Pull apart! Pull . . . *apart*!"

The garden drew them, held them for moments only before the room jerked them back. Garden again now, and room again, and garden, room, garden, room, this way and that, entangled, entwined, one body, one life, one hist—

"No! We're two! Concentrate! We're *different*!"

Time freezes. Two rooms divide, slowly.

"I think it's working."

"Yes."

"Oh—wait!"

They reach for bags dropped in the snow.

"Okay! Now! *Separate*!"

About them: furnishings, books, pictures, favored relics of childhood.

The wrong ones.

But never mind, they can always . . .

Small cracking sound. Collapse. Disintegration. In separate bedrooms, universes apart, perfection shatters beyond hope, stranding them.

In the wrong realities.

"Oh, no. No."

Wrong lives.

_____Day One

Sitting in Naia's chair beside the tidy little heap of glass and wood on the bookcase, Alaric barely heard the knock. When the door opened he didn't move. No point. No escape route.

"Oh, you are here. Why didn't you answer? Listen, you know the . . . "

Whatever she'd come in for was forgotten at once. She stared blankly at the face gazing helplessly back at her. Their eyes locked, and when they locked it was impossible for either of them to look away, or even blink. But then Alaric saw something at the corner of his eye. A shifting, a changing. Shapes and colors reorganizing themselves all around them. Only when the room became still again were they able to blink. The blink unlocked their stare. Alaric looked about him. Naia's things were gone. Her clothes, the dressing gown behind the door, the old toys and dolls, her makeup and jewelry, posters, magazines, the multitude of mobiles, all the strategically placed candles and incense sticks. Everything that was particular to Naia Underwood had either faded out of existence or turned into male equivalents. Even the wallpaper, curtains, and duvet cover had become more "Alaric." He was marveling at this, trying to understand, when Alex gave a small shiver, and laughed.

"Someone walking over my grave," she said.

She seemed unperturbed by the changes. Not even faintly surprised. Until:

"That isn't the Folly. Oh, what happened?"

Alaric remained seated, too confused to even consider an answer. Why did it no longer look like Naia's room? Why wasn't her mother demanding to know what he was doing there?

"Oh, Alaric. I should never have let you have it up here."

She'd called him Alaric. How did she know his name? And what did she mean, she should never have let him—

She whirled on him, face knotted with fury.

"Well? Nothing to say for yourself?"

He shrank from her. He'd forgotten how formidable she could be when she lost her temper.

"And what are you doing up here with your boots on? Boots with *snow* on them? In your *room*? Alaric, what is this? What are you *playing* at? Honest to God, boy, it's about time you started behaving responsibly! I sometimes think you haven't the sense you were born with. I am so . . . so *disappointed* in you!"

And Naia's former mother rushed out in tears.

1.2a

Naia was alone in Alaric's room when his things vanished or changed into hers. She saw his room transmogrify into a tattier, sadder version of her own, complete with mobiles, but fewer of them, and dustier. Very much alarmed, anxious to see beyond the room without knowing why, she opened the door—and stifled a scream. For there stood a gawky, brightly dressed stranger with startled hair and jewelry that looked as if it had been fashioned by a bricklayer with a hangover. "Naia," the scary stranger said, "are you planning on finishing the Escher, or shall I put it away?" With no idea what this apparition was talking about, Naia mumbled something unintelligible and closed the door fast. She leaned against it, understanding everything in a rush of dread. Lexie's Folly was smashed. There was no way back. She was stuck here for good, and Alaric's reality had adapted to take account of this. Of her. The woman outside the door, the aunt obviously, thought she'd always known her when she'd only ever *heard* of her a minute ago. For the aunt, and everyone else here, Alaric Underwood had never existed. There had only ever been Naia.

As soon as she felt that her legs would support her

she went downstairs. Careful to avoid the aunt, she put on her coat and boots (which were waiting for her in Alaric's gloomy hall) and opened the front door. Very much preoccupied as she stepped into the drive, she was slow to hear the dry slithering sound from somewhere above. Only when the slithering became a muffled clatter did she look up—and jump aside just in time. Not quite far enough though.

A loose slate glanced off her shoulder and thudded into the snow at her feet. She stared at the triangular indentation in the material of her coat. If she hadn't moved when she did the slate would have pierced her skull. She stepped well away from the house, unnerved by the thought that there might now be a new reality, seconds old, in which a Naia Underwood who had not been quick enough lay on the ground, blood oozing from her head into the snow.

1.3a

Alaric had walked around the garden several times. He needed unconfined thinking space and the garden had plenty of that, with enough idiosyncratic cover to escape idle glances from the windows of the house. "I'm here to stay," he said to himself as he plodded. "I'm *here*. To *stay*." There would be no going back. Kate Faraday would not be moving in. There was no heartbreaking grave here, no Aunt Liney. Pity about Liney; she wasn't so bad once you got to know her. Well, can't have everything.

For the most part his eyes were on the ground just ahead of him, taking little note of where he trod. When he found that his feet had delivered him to the roots of the Family Tree he stopped abruptly and stepped back. He dare not go too near the tree. He might finish up anywhere. Might even land back in his own reality. He turned about. Walked quickly away.

1.4a

The last of the snow was falling by the time Naia climbed the cemetery steps. At the top she paused, trying to find the courage to do what she knew she must. She stepped toward the nearest headstone and brushed the snow away. The revealed name meant nothing to her. She went to the next, and the next, and so on, dashing snow from inscription after inscription. By the time she'd read eighteen her hands were like ice. But when she saw the nineteenth epitaph, in the cloister of ivy under the wall, she ceased to feel the cold.

ALEXANDRA UNDERWOOD

BELOVED WIFE AND MOTHER

1966–2003

It should have helped knowing that it wasn't really her mother's grave, but it didn't, much. Her mother was still very much alive, but she would never see her face again, never have a laugh with her or fall out with her and make up. Never again would they go shopping together, or snuggle up on the couch looking through clothes catalogs or watching the moronic game shows that drove Dad out of the room tearing at the remains of his hair. Life without Mum. How could she bear it? With this thought, finally, the tears came. Great, gushing, shoulder-heaving welts of tears.

"You all right there?"

She turned. A man in a black overcoat stood in the watery blur, about where the path should be.

"Yes." She turned away again, embarrassed to be caught grieving.

"You sure?"

"Oh, shove off," she said quietly.

Not quietly enough. "Right you are," the man said.

She glanced along the line of her shoulder and watched him walk away. He had an odd stride, young and old at the same time. There was something sad about him that was hard to pin down. Something lost and hopeless. She was ashamed. He hadn't been prying. Just passing, heard her sobbing, offered his concern. She wiped her eyes on her sleeve.

"Sorry!" she shouted. "Didn't mean that!"

The man stopped; appeared to be considering his response. Evidently deciding, he started back toward her. Naia groaned. Why couldn't she keep her trap shut? Drawing near, the snow grunting beneath his feet, the man stuck a hand into one of his deep pockets.

"Aniseed ball?"

"Pardon?"

He tugged a soiled paper bag out of the pocket and twitched it open with knobbly blue fingers as he joined her. She peered in.

"No, thanks. Bad for your teeth."

This must have amused him, for he grinned. His teeth looked surprisingly good for their age, and for someone so keen on sweets. He popped two aniseed balls into his mouth, creating bulges in both badly shaven cheeks, and shoved the bag back in his pocket. He mumbled something she didn't catch. Wishing that she didn't feel an obligation to be so courteous, she asked him to repeat it. He shuffled the contents of his mouth.

"I said it's peaceful here."

It's a graveyard, she thought. What do you expect, exotic dancers and strobe lighting? "Yes," she said.

"Me and my mates used to play here," the man said. "Seems like yesterday. Climb the trees, hide among the stones, just larking about, like. You know. No harm."

In spite of his rather grizzled appearance and dour demeanor, there was something incongruously youthful about the old man. The uncertain way he moved, fluttered his hands, glanced about, eyes everywhere.

"Wasn't your mother, was she?"

"My mother?" He was looking at the grave. She shuddered. "No." Rather too emphatically.

But the implication remained. And it was true, here. This was her mother's grave as far as everyone here was concerned. She would have to acknowledge it before long. But could she, should she, simply because others believed it? Live her life as if her mother had died, when she knew that she had not?

The old man crunched hard on an aniseed ball and tilted his head like a bird to look at her. "I've seen you, I have."

"Seen me?"

"Oh yes. Many times." He tapped his left temple. "In here."

She plunged her icy hands into her pockets. "What do you mean?"

He didn't answer. Instead: "What's your name?"

She twigged. How could she have been so naïve? This old perv hung around places like this, hoping some young girl—or boy, probably wasn't fussy—would come along so he could chat her up and God knew what else. She stepped back, away from him, and the grave.

"Why don't you tell me *your* name?" she said sharply.

She didn't give a damn what his name was, but the cemetery was just across the lane from her old school playground. This character might get his jollies from hanging around near it. If anything dodgy happened once the kids were back from vacation the police might be glad of a name.

Again he did not respond to the direct question. He started back the way he'd been going when she made the mistake of apologizing. Her contempt for him burgeoned.

"What is it, a secret?" she shouted after him.

"Secret?" she heard him mumble, and laugh very lightly: "Secret!"

She watched him go, welcoming each footprint in the snow that took him farther from her. When he reached the steps he turned; half turned. Naia prepared to walk quickly away, even run, if he started back toward her a second time. But he made no move to do so. Instead, he spoke. With the air so still his words, though quietly spoken, were perfectly clear.

"My name's Aldous. Aldous Underwood. The one and only."

He bowed low, with the flourish of a stage magician, descended the steps, and was gone.

1.5a

Alaric sat in the room that had been Naia's, in the chair he'd seen in three realities. The family album was spread across his knees. This time it was his own album, not hers, and as he'd brought it with him from the garden it had not changed, unlike the room. Everything in his album fitted perfectly here now, except the empty pages that should contain pictures from the past two years. He imagined that Naia's mother, once she'd gotten over the accident, had put some pictures on those pages, but in his album there were none at all. How could he ever explain that? Should he hide the book away, claim to know nothing of it, so that its disappearance would eventually become one of life's unsolved mysteries? Naia was lucky, in this if nothing else. His father never opened the album; didn't even know for sure where it was kept.

The missing two years were going to give him other headaches too. Naia's brain contained all the memories her former parents would now expect to be in his. There would be times when things they'd done together as a family and with friends would be mentioned, require comment, or at least some recollection. He gulped at the thought of all the making it up as he went along that he would have to do.

But this was a small price to pay, and nothing compared to what Naia would have to contend with. When his ex-father returned from Newcastle his memory would tell him that he was *her* father, that he had never had a son, only a daughter: a daughter with whom he'd shared a terrible loss. No one there would know that her grief was just beginning. There was nothing Alaric could do about that, but he hoped she didn't think he was sitting here in her house, her room, thrilled by the upturn in his fortunes at the expense of hers.

And yet . . .

An exquisite glow washed through him. Down in the kitchen, in the farthest reaches of the house from his room overlooking the river, Alex Underwood was preparing a special meal for her husband's return— and for her son. The house radiated a warmth and color it had never lost here, and all was very right with the world. They were going to be a real family again. The three of them. Just like the old days.

1.6a

The old days were coming back. Slowly, gradually, but coming. Aldous could recall little of the village or the adjoining town, but there was more each day of the house and his life there when his body was young. In one of these new memories he raced from room to

room, hiding from his little sisters and brother. His
sisters had high excited voices.

There was one room in particular: the corner room
up there on the right. There'd been wooden shutters at
the windows back then. Maroon shutters with slats. He
had first remembered the room a week ago, standing on
this very spot across the river. There'd been someone at
the window, a young man, who must have reminded
him of himself, for his former occupancy of the room
had returned to him in an instant, with some force.
Aldous longed to enter that room again and gaze down
at the slow river as he once had, a lifetime ago. The river
had been thick with lily pads when the view was his.
Lilies and shutters: such incidental things. How many
more incidentals were due to come home to roost?

A few days ago he'd remembered his grandmother
and been filled with a rich and wonderful warmth. A
small fleshy woman full of kindness and laughter. He
recalled sitting on her knee while she read to him, and
on the kitchen table in his underclothes while she
washed him with the softest of flannels from a white

tin bowl. The washing water had come from the rain barrel outside the kitchen door, heated in a copper pan on the range. The seven o'clock news always seemed to be on the wireless when Gran was washing him. Much talk of the war effort.

Night had fallen, but it was as light beside the river as any winter night in his limited memory. Gazing across at the house where he was sure he'd been happy once, Aldous felt a sudden need to be nearer to it. There was nothing between him and the house but the river's width. He stepped down onto the snow-covered ice and tested it with one foot. It held. He lowered his other foot. The ice barely moved. He started across, step by cautious step. If it cracked and opened up, he would drown or freeze to death. He would not be missed. There was no one now. This, if nothing else, he was sure of.

He reached the halfway point, and stopped. Standing on the frozen river in the glowing darkness was like standing between two worlds. He remained there for some time, trying to decide which way to go:

back to the bank, where he was a rootless stranger, or forward, across the ice, to his childhood home. The scene of his death sixty years earlier.

1.7a

Naia sat in the room that had been Alaric's, in the chair that was the same in both realities. The family album was spread across her knees. Soon she would have to remove those last seven or eight pages, put them where no one would think of looking. She couldn't destroy them. She could never destroy them. They were all she had left of . . .

It had to be faced up to. She no longer had a mother. Again. *I no longer have a mother.* How was that for blunt acceptance? Whatever she did from now on, wherever she went, she would always know that her mother was going about her life elsewhere—without her. The woman who had given birth to her no longer knew that she'd ever had a daughter. She wouldn't be remembered for a second. She struggled not to blub her eyes out yet again. What a day of secret tears and sorrow! What a conclusion to all that had happened! To be stuck for life in a world she hadn't known existed until a week ago!

As she saw it, she had two choices. Two alternatives which, for once, were quite transparent. She could spend her days moping and sulking and hating the world for this devastating twist; or she could try and make the best of things. She entertained the first option for very little time. There was no point in despising Alaric for stealing her life—he hadn't intended to—or in giving Kate Faraday a hard time for being there instead of her mother. They weren't the enemy. The only enemy was herself if she gave in to such things.

The clang of the doorbell filled the house. This was it. The moment. She returned the album to the shopping bag, shoved it under the bed that used to be Alaric's, and went out to the landing. Her heart was pounding. She looked down. She couldn't see all the way along the hall, but she heard the aunt open the front door, cry a greeting, and Alaric's father's "I don't know, locked out of my own house."

"Safety precaution," the aunt said.

There followed a brief discussion about the state of the roads, then introductions—Kate and the aunt, the aunt and Kate—and the sound of feet stomping on the mat, and Ivan asking what was burning and where all the warmth was coming from, and "Stone me." Naia couldn't hear every word and wasn't really interested, until: "That daughter of yours. What a slave driver. And talk about perfectionist."

"Where is she anyway?"

And there it was. Unconditional acceptance of a daughter he'd never met. Alaric no longer existed for him. Never had. She saw the alternate version of her father step into the hall. He was the spitting image of the one she'd known all her life, except for being a bit scruffier and in need of a haircut. Kate and the aunt were right behind him. Kate saw her first.

"Naia!"

The warmth of her voice. Absolutely genuine. Nothing false or self-serving about Kate Faraday. She'd always known this, as her mother had. Kate would never have entertained anything more than a mild flirtation with Ivan if Alex had still been alive.

And then the other two were looking up as well, beaming. It was like the closing scene of some slushy film or TV drama where everything comes out right in the end. Comes out right. If they only knew. She couldn't find any words. The best she could manage was a small wave as she walked to the head of the stairs. Well, here goes, she thought, gripping the banister rail. The old wood, recently polished by her and others, was strangely reassuring. She needed all the reassurance she could get. She was on her own now. Totally alone in a world of strangers with familiar faces. As she went down, making the most of the rail's support, there was a peculiar tightness in her chest. A lump in her throat as big as a house.

A CRACK IN THE LINE

THE WITHERN RISE TRILOGY · VOLUME I

The Mysterious Ways of Chance

A House by the River

Michael Lawrence: A Life of Sorts

What Happens Next?

An Introduction from the Author

Recently I realized that I've long been fascinated by moments in time. My fascination was initially by way of photography. From about the age of ten, with my first camera, and later as a young photographer in London, I was enthralled by the idea of freezing instants that could never be repeated and never be captured by anyone else in quite the same way. Later still, I would write many poems about an instant observed, experienced, or felt in passing. These days my interest in fleeting moments is finding expression in the Withern Rise trilogy. In these novels—a continuing story, really—I'm very much concerned with the way a life can switch tracks following a hesitation, a faltering step, the checking of a door. The life-changing indifference of Chance is one of the driving forces behind the trilogy.

My own life has gone off on any number of unpremeditated tangents, most of which I haven't a hope of identifying. One that I can certainly pick out occurred one spring evening in the 1960s, when I was 21. I was staying in the house of an Austro-Hungarian baroness of my acquaintance, who had offered me the use of her home on the condition that I feed her cat. In order to feed the cat (and myself anything but cat food), I had to find work, so I took a laboring job at a factory that made window casements. It wasn't the kind of work that left you with a sigh of accomplishment at the end of the day. I can't say how long I would have stayed in that job or that house, or what I'd

3

have done next, if not for a phone call from JB, a friend of mine. JB phoned to tell me about an ad he'd seen in which Butlin's, a holiday company, was advertising for photographers for the forthcoming summer season. Suddenly I had two alternatives: spend the summer hauling window frames through a gloomy factory, or strut about in the sun day after day, on beaches, where there would be girls with very little on. It wasn't an easy decision (!), but once I'd made it a whole new reality kicked in.

And here's the point. If not for that casual phone call—or if I hadn't acted upon it—four marriages would not have taken place, five children (to date) would not have been born, I would not have lived in any of the thirty or more places I have lived in, and by direct or indirect association, a great many other lives would have gone in very different directions. That phone call, those few words, changed histories, led to my writing the Withern Rise trilogy, and my telling you about it here. But such things aren't unique to me. Like mine, your life—and the lives of many others—would have gone any number of different ways if not for a phone call, a change of mind, any number of tiny things. Because of things you've done, or not done, people have been born, entire lives have been shaped or altered. Scary, isn't it?

—Michael Lawrence

A House by the River

Until a couple of years ago I always thought that I would spend my declining summer evenings strolling along the shore of some quiet coastal town while a fat old sun sinks slowly below a glittering horizon. But then, one day, it occurred to me that it isn't a coast I should settle beside in my fast-approaching dotage, but a quiet stretch of river deep in the country. I was eating a sandwich on a bench by just such a stretch at the edge of a certain Cambridgeshire village where I'd come to seek the former home of a famous children's author. The day was warm and golden, a low breeze shuffled the reeds, willows draped the water, and as I sat there I realized that it was a very long time since I'd felt so at ease, so content.

The house I'd come to find was, and is, called The Manor. In one guise or another, The Manor played a part in almost all the novels of Lucy M. Boston, its best-known incarnation being 'Green Knowe.' Lucy Boston bought The Manor in 1939 and died there in 1990 at the age of 97. In her early days there she removed several latter-day windows and structures, restored hidden rooms, uncovered old fireplaces, doorways, and floors, discovering in the process, to her delight, that parts of the original building dated back to Norman times. She came to love the house so much that when she started writing at the age of 60 it seemed a natural setting for her stories. Thus she added a history of her own to its already ancient fabric.

My own sudden longing for a riverside house is easily explained. I was born in one. It still stands beside the same river as The Manor, and not so many miles away. The modest Victorian mansion in which I spent the first four or five years of my life was my grandparents' house. Today it stands neglected and dull, in an unkempt garden with fallen fences, rusting vehicles dumped near the back kitchen, but once upon a time—of course!—it was a grand place, ivy-covered, with smoke tumbling from the tall chimneys, bedroom windows with creaking shutters overlooking the lily-covered river. We had a gardener who told me what the multitudes of berries and nuts were called. There was light and laughter and we had a great many visitors. We kept chickens and goats, and my older cousin, who lived there too, had a pony. On occasional Sundays there were family picnics in punts on the river.

It seems odd to me now, but I'd never previously attempted to write about that house, except in a very long poem published many years ago in an obscure magazine (and rewritten a hundred times since). But that day, minutes before I entered the grounds of The Manor for the first time, I decided that my own childhood home was the ideal setting for the trilogy I was planning. And so it became. That old house is now Withern Rise, where all the comings and goings in parallel and not-so-parallel realities of The Aldous Lexicon take place. Like Lucy Boston, I've made a fiction of a house and garden that has played a very important part in my life. I find this strangely pleasing.

The real-life inspiration for Withern Rise

Michael Lawrence

A Life of Sorts

When I was ten or so, equally fascinated by the night sky and ancient artifacts, I thought I might become either an astronomer or an archaeologist when I was old enough. It didn't happen. I went to art school instead. I stayed at art school for just two years before taking a job in a London design studio, where I began training as a graphic designer. It wasn't long, however, before I discovered a greater aptitude for photography. By the age of twenty I was a freelance photographer whose clients included national newspapers, magazine publishers, and advertising agencies. I took pictures of politicians, pop stars, underwear, and model girls (plus a few real ones). While working as a photographer I was also writing, and somewhere along the line I realized that I wanted to write more than take vacuous snaps, so one December day I abandoned everything I owned (an apartment full of furniture) and went to Paris to try my hand at starving while typing. As it turned out, I had a gift for this.

Years later, after a sprinkling of adventures, encounters, and a lot of changes of address, I moved to a big unheated

Georgian house in the country and opened an antiques shop and art gallery. At the top of the house there was a three-roomed attic. I used one room as a darkroom, another as a painting studio, the third as a study. In the study I wrote things. In 1995, after thirty years of failing to convince editors that I had anything to offer, I finally had a novel published. Since that first novel I've published nine more, plus half a dozen picture books for young children, adaptations of Victorian classics, and more than twenty short stories. I've also adapted two of my books for radio and my radio serial, "Is There Life in Other Heads?," was broadcast by the BBC in 2004.

But I still want to be an astronomer or an archaeologist when I grow up.

Recommended Reading

Until five or six years ago, I would never go out without a paperback novel in my pocket. These days, however, that defeats me for some reason, and I'm drawn to biographies and popular science rather than fiction. But here's a short selection of books that gave me great pleasure in my early years as a struggling writer.

The Cook by Harry Kressing. Why isn't this novel celebrated as the classic it is? Read it and be captivated!

Pictures of Fidelman by Bernard Malamud. I think I read all of Malamud's novels, but this is the one I'm fondest of.

The Ginger Man by J. P. Donleavy. As heavily influenced by James Joyce as Donleavy obviously was in the writing of this book, what words and imagery were spun here! It took me ten years to crawl out from under the influence of Donleavy's and Malamud's ways with words.

The Foundation Trilogy by Isaac Asimov. For me, this trilogy is the greatest of all sci-fi storytelling. Years after he finished it, Asimov and other writers wrote additional Foundation novels—much longer books, all of which lack the pace and presence of these three originals. The current trend toward long books highlights the curse of the computer. Previously the author, using a typewriter, would hammer out the most 'direct' book he could in order to get on with his life. Now, nothing is thrown away; it's just refined, and the refinement process drains the life out of stories. In my own writing I pare down and down, preferring to simplify rather than expand, believing (rightly or wrongly) that this will make for a more engrossing read.

Among more recent favorite writers is Raymond Carver, his poems in particular. I think it's the directness of Carver's approach, the intimate way he records tiny incidents, that clicks with me.

An excerpt from SMALL ETERNITIES,
Withern Rise Trilogy • Volume II

Wednesday: 9

Naia often went into the garden when she had some problem to resolve, but walking through high water was hard
work, so when she came to the upturned rowing boat on the
slope above the dock she welcomed it as a place to sit. The
repetitive call of a pigeon on the roof, and evening light like
old parchment, soothed her. At certain times, and this was
undoubtedly one of them, the garden at Withern Rise felt as
solitary as any place on earth. Naia had never been afraid of
solitude, but tonight she would have valued company. Alaric's
company. She needed to talk about the things on her mind.
She imagined they were on his mind, too, though she could-
n't be sure. Alaric still seemed to keep himself to himself, suspicious of fanciful flights of the imagination, inspired conclu-
sions. Even so, likely as he was to be unpleasant and snide
rather than amiable and chatty, he was still the only person
anywhere who wouldn't think she was stark staring bonkers to
talk of such things.

Separately, they'd got enough information out of the old
family album to convince them of who they'd met in the other
reality. Most of the photos were untitled, undated, but they

had come across two with the name Rayner written underneath. One was of a putty-faced baby in a crocheted shawl and someone's arms; the other of a boy of four or five sitting on the garden swing, an older sister standing beside him, frowning for the lens. It was a third picture that clinched it. This one was captioned: The Floods, June 1945. Here, the boy sat on his father's shoulders. The man wore high rubber waders, and stood in water that reached his groin, a small paper bag in one hand. They both waved and smiled up at the camera, situated somewhere above them. There was no doubt in Naia's mind, or Alaric's now. The small boy who had found them so fascinating that morning was the grandfather they'd last seen five years ago, aged sixty-two, on his premature deathbed. The man whose shoulders he rode, in whose song he had joined, was their great-grandfather, Alaric Eldon.

Sitting on the boat, gazing across a lake that had been a river all her life, thoughts tumbled through Naia's head like loaded dice. Three times, she and Alaric had visited another period of time, not an alternate reality-unless time was another form of reality. There was scope here for considerable contemplation, but what interested her more for the moment was one of the people they'd met there. Not her grandfather, but his older brother, Aldous. In the cemetery of her old reality there was a grave whose headstone declared that an Aldous Underwood was buried there. The year of death was given as 1945. She assumed-because it was all she could do without more precise information-that he had been eleven when he died. If the Aldous whose bones lay beneath that stone was the one with the boat, he'd had very little time to live when she and Alaric met him. He hadn't looked like someone about to snuff it from some illness or disease, which suggested that something happened in the weeks or months following their meeting. Something, fatal.

After a while she got up and walked along the bank, stooping occasionally to trail her hands in the water. She was puzzled by her earlier fatigue. She'd felt dopey enough after the other trips, but this time she'd been totally knocked out. Why? When she'd passed from her reality into Alaric's back in February, there'd been the most appalling pain, but it had stopped as soon as she arrived there. There'd been no pain before these recent visits, hardly any sensation at all, but when she returned! So what was the difference? Well, there was one quite obvious difference. There'd been no time differential between her reality and Alaric's. They lived parallel existences, minute for minute; but the recent journeys had been to another day. Another decade. She smiled. Naia Underwood: Time Traveler. It was a short-lived smile. Whatever it was about the trips to 1945 that brought about such dreadful feebleness, she didn't fancy experiencing it again in a hurry. Curious as she was about life at Withern Rise back then, she would not be shinning up that tree for a day or two.

The tree. The envelope in the message hole. With so much going on it had slipped her mind. She rounded the corner of the house and entered the south garden. At the Family Tree she removed the envelope. As she was doing so she had the oddest feeling of being watched, and turned just in time to see binoculars lowered amid the bushes and trees along the drive. She glimpsed a face. A man's. A stranger's.

"Excuse me?" she said loudly.

He said nothing; scurried away. She heard him splashing toward the gate. Now what was he up to?

She shrugged. In summer, people often darted up the drive for a peep at the house, not because it was particularly striking or grand, but simply because it was there. Such intrusions were taken for granted without being welcomed, but for someone with no business there to broach the drive when it was underwater suggested an even greater degree of nosiness than usual. And he had binoculars. Peeping Tom? She would have to warn Kate.

Reaching the house, Naia climbed in the window, a routine mode of entry by now, and removed the waders. A minute later, up in her room, she broke the seal of the envelope. Inside, she found a folded sheet of paper covered in typing. Same primitive manual typewriter as before, but she'd been wrong about the content. It wasn't the same at all.

Warning

Entire worlds, whole universes, identical in most prominent details, coexist within a hair's breadth of one another. The realities go about the construction of their histories without any more awareness of each other than a flea is aware of communication satellites.

This is just as well.

Imagine if we all knew that alternate versions of ourselves were washing their hair at the instant we were washing ours, eating a boiled egg when we were eating one, or, for that matter, sitting on the lavatory while we were taking a shower. For the most part the realities do not overlap or encroach, but there are some that draw you into them. These are almost always earlier realities that continue to exist when standard time moves on.

They are dangerous. Resist them if you can.

Aldous U.
Withern Rise